HP

D0130189

Richmond upon Thames Libraries

Renew online at www.richmond.gov.uk/libraries

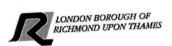

LONDON BOROUGH OF
RICHMOND UPON THAMES

While the events described and some of the characters in this book may be based on actual historical events and real people, Daphne Rowntree is a fictional character, created by the author, and her diary is a work of fiction.

Scholastic Children's Books,
Euston House, 24 Eversholt Street,
London NW1 1DB, UK

A division of Scholastic Ltd
London ~ New York ~ Toronto ~ Sydney ~ Auckland
Mexico City ~ New Delhi ~ Hong Kong

First published in the UK by Scholastic Ltd, 2008
This edition published by Scholastic Ltd, 2015

Text © Valerie Wilding, 2008
Cover photography © Jeff Cottenden, 2015

ISBN 978 1407 15661 3

Typeset by M Rules
Printed and bound in the UK by CPI Group (UK) Ltd, Croydon, CR0 4YY

2 4 6 8 10 9 7 5 3 1

The right of Valerie Wilding and Jeff Cottenden to be identified
as the author and cover photographer of this work respectively has been asserted by
them in accordance with the Copyright, Designs and Patents Act, 1988.

Papers used by Scholastic Children's Books are made from woods grown in sustainable forests.

www.scholastic.co.uk

1916 Christmas Day

I'm getting fearfully slack. When war broke out, I vowed to keep a diary, so that one day I could tell my children what it was like. And when my mother asked me, just last month, how it was going, all I could say was, "Not very well, Mimi. In fact, it's not going at all. I'll start it tomorrow, most definitely I will."

"Daffy, darling," she said, "if you don't want to do it, don't do it."

That's my mother all over. But I do want to do it and, lo and behold, I've begun (even though a month has gone by since I said I'd start the next day). One of my Christmas presents was this beautiful book. I love the pale pink silk cover and the creamy pages, and today seems the perfect day for starting something new. However, I can't think what else to write, so, as it's a lovely crisp afternoon, I'll go for a ride on Honeycomb. I have a Christmas present for her – a thick rug to keep her warm.

28th December

Gosh, so much has happened. The very very *very* worst thing is that Papa has been badly injured and is in hospital in France. Mimi is going wild with worry.

"If only Charles had stayed in London," she moaned to my Aunt Leonora, who's here for Christmas and New Year. "Why did he go to war? He was working for the government. He didn't need to go to France. Why? Your Cecil has stayed."

Aunt Leonora said firmly, "My husband has a bad chest. You're his sister, so you know that very well. Anyway, he's doing important work here. I know I'm lucky that he comes home to me every night, but you must remember that Charles felt he needed to go to war."

"Aunt Leonora's right, Mimi," I said. "Papa's frightfully patriotic."

"I know," she sighed. "He's fighting for England."

I didn't argue, but I think she means he's fighting for France, because when all's said and done, that's where the Germans are doing their worst. At least I think it is. It's very confusing. I can't really tell whether they're in Belgium or France, to be honest. They have this imaginary line they call the "front" and that's where a lot of the fighting is. Either way, the Germans shouldn't be in either France or Belgium.

Gosh, I hope they don't invade us! A battle at a place called Verdun, in France, ended only a week or so ago, and it had been going on since February! Imagine if that was happening here, in our peaceful corner of England. We've been lucky, so far, but I know there have been bombs dropped from aeroplanes on to London. And, of course, those hideous airships, the Zeppelins, have managed to bomb and kill nearly 300 people this year.

It seems a very dangerous sort of war. All the ones I've read of in history books have been about men on horseback making charges, and having skirmishes and what not. In those you only got killed if you were face to face with the enemy. But in this war, they fire shells and use machine guns and drop bombs from the air, and it's all just awful. The word "shell" didn't sound too dreadful to me at first, so I looked it up, and it turns out to be a metal container with explosives inside. I suppose that when it lands, it explodes. Horrible. Hundreds and hundreds of thousands of men have been killed in the last two years of war, Papa told us in his last letter. Horses, too, which I cannot bear to think about.

But let us hope that our new Prime Minister, Mr David Lloyd George, can do what Mr Asquith couldn't: bring us safely through this war, to victory.

I'll pray especially hard for Papa tonight. Aunt Leonora

says there are terrific nurses out there in France and Belgium. I hope they look after him.

I'm letting my darling dog, Billie, sleep on my bed tonight. He's such a comfort when I'm anxious, and I'm sad he's growing old. I don't know why everybody doesn't have an Airedale. He's the nicest, most polite dog, and so handsome.

31st December

On the way to church, I decided that all my prayers would be for Papa. The weather's atrocious at the front. Men suffer the worst conditions imaginable in their trenches, everyone says. They're constantly standing in icy water and thick mud. I'm frightened for Papa, but I'm also scared that when he comes home, his ship might be sunk by an evil German U-boat, gliding through the sea beneath them.

Before we went in, the vicar sought me out and said I needn't sing in the choir today if I didn't want to, in view of my worries.

"I can't let them down," I said. "I shall sing."

"But Miss Rowntree," he said, "we'll manage perfectly well. You shouldn't take on too much."

"I insist," I said, and took my place. Behind me, I heard

him heave a heavy sigh. I know why. It's my voice. Even *I* am aware it's pretty awful – much too loud – but I do love to sing.

I prayed so hard for Papa during silent prayer that I didn't notice when the rest of the choir stood. You'd think someone might have nudged me!

I love being in the choir. The other members are mainly from the village, and tend to stick together, but I don't mind being the odd one out. Truly I don't. I just love to sing out with all my heart!

2nd January 1917

We have had the worst news possible. My darling Papa has died.

3rd January

There's so much to do, and we are all too upset to cope. Thank goodness Aunt Leonora's here. Uncle Cecil's coming down at the weekend to help with the arrangements.

My young brother and sister are being looked after so tenderly by Miss Rowan, their governess. May says she will embroider a new handkerchief for Mimi, because all hers are being used up. Freddie says he will look after us all until Archie comes home.

Archie! My poor brother. He spent New Year with a school friend's family in the West Country, where the dreadful news was broken to him. He's on his way home today. He's due to leave school altogether very soon. Perhaps he won't return there. Perhaps he'll stay here and be the man of the house and help look after everything.

4th January

Archie was late home last night and was very late to breakfast this morning. Fortunately, Mrs Rose, our cook, expected him to be tired and kept everything hot for him. He didn't eat much, though.

After he'd gone upstairs to supervise Elsie unpacking his luggage, Mimi cried herself into a puddle. "I just don't know how I'm going to look after everything," she sobbed.

Our estate isn't huge compared to some others – just the gardens, the parkland and lakes, the woods, two farms and some cottages, and a couple of larger houses – but there is still much to do, and Papa knew about it all.

"When Papa went to France, he said you should leave everything to the staff," I reminded Mimi. "They know what they're doing."

Even so, there are always decisions to be made, and normally Mimi would write to Papa for advice. She's a bit like me about decisions – I can't even decide what to have for breakfast.

Oh dear.

When Archie reappeared, he found me staring out of the window, twiddling the curtain.

"Are you all right, Daffers, old thing?" he asked quietly.

"Not really," I said, and told him about Mimi's concerns over the estate.

"When I've finished my education, I shall look after the estate," he said firmly. "In the meantime, I suppose we can always get someone to manage it for us. I'll talk to Uncle Cecil at the weekend."

Why didn't I think of that?

7th January

Papa's body has been returned to us. The funeral is arranged for Monday. I don't think I can bear it.

9th January

Today we buried my Papa. It was awful. May sobbed so hard that my throat went lumpy, and I thought I might start weeping. But I was determined not to. Mimi was strong. At least, she looked strong – yet frail at the same time. Afterwards, Freddie was so sweet and played the big (well, quite big) brother perfectly, for once. "Come on, May," he said. "Buck up. I've seen an otter in the lake. Let's go and find it."

May shuddered. "Ugh." She hates nature. He took her off to play in the nursery instead.

When I went to my room to dress for dinner I did, at last, have a little cry. And so, I swear, did Elsie. I'm lucky to have such a sweet maid. Mimi's is a tyrant.

12th January

This morning, Mimi asked to see me after breakfast. I went to her room just as her tray was being removed. She'd eaten very little. I felt guilty for stuffing down sausages *and* ham (decisions again!) but this is the first day since we heard of Papa's death that I've felt like eating at all. An early morning ride certainly wakens the appetite.

"Daffy, darling," she said. "Archie's going back to school to sit his last exams, so I'll need your help until Cecil finds me an estate manager. I know your father said the staff can manage, but they're bound to *ask* me things, and I'm sure I shan't know the answers."

"You will, Mimi," I told her. "You probably don't realize how much you do know about the estate. After all, you listened to Papa over the breakfast table for all those years. You must admit," I said, daringly, "he did go on..."

She laughed! "On and on! You're absolutely right, Daffy." Her forehead wrinkled. "But you will help me, won't you?"

Of course I promised. But when it comes to the estate and the farms and everything, I honestly don't have a clue. I always have a book on my lap at breakfast.

I hate myself a little bit tonight, because for a while today I felt angry at Papa for leaving us like this.

What sort of a horrible person am I?

20th January

We're all still so unhappy. Whenever we meet on the stairs or in the corridors, we look at each other and the tears start to leak out again. But today, when it happened, we actually laughed at ourselves.

Unhappy we may be, but the pain eases a tiny bit each day. Some nice people call on Mimi every couple of days. I am so pleased. Like me, she doesn't have many friends. With her, it's mainly because she works at her painting for such long hours. With me, I honestly think it's because people's mothers don't really approve of me. I once overheard Elizabeth Baguley's mother saying, "Daphne is such a *tomboy*. She's always spent so much time racing around with Archibald and his friends, so I suppose it's hardly surprising. She can never just ride anywhere – she has to gallop. And whoever heard of a girl of her age climbing trees?"

Well, I don't care. Archie will be home for good at the end of term! Mimi wants him back as soon as he's finished his exams. His school's too close to the south coast for her liking. She says she can't sleep at night for fear a German bomb might burst through the school roof into Archie's little study. She wants him back here where, thank goodness, the war scarcely touches us. Oh, I cannot wait! Even when he goes up to university, he won't be far from home at all! Though I'm a little older than him, I love his company.

21st January

I returned from a ride on Honeycomb this morning to find our housekeeper, Mrs Hallibert, hopping about in a lather, and Freddie being taken upstairs by Miss Rowan, roaring his head off that he hadn't done it, whatever it was.

He was in trouble for doing something naughty with a pair of scissors and a tray cloth.

Mrs Hallibert, who is *very* forward sometimes, stood, hands on hips, watching them go upstairs. "You should keep a closer eye on those children, Miss Rowan," she said.

I whipped my boots off before she saw how muddy they were. When she turned her face was like thunder. "And who's going to keep a sharp eye on you now your father's gone, Miss Daphne, eh?"

I couldn't believe she'd spoken to me like that. I raced upstairs and burst into tears. I know she's known me all my life, but she should stick to housekeeping, should Mrs Hallibert. She has a point, though. I'm almost certain to have a little more freedom now. Poor dear Papa never liked me gallivanting off on my own, or with Archie and his friends.

Mimi will soon return to her painting, and it's clear the servants have enough to do running the house and keeping tabs on Freddie and May. They won't even notice me. Apart from Mrs Hallibert, who misses *nothing*, most people don't notice me. At least, they seem not to.

22nd January

Oh dear, our first major problem. One of the stable lads, Troggs, has left us. Although he's of the age when he should go and fight for our country, he can't, because he's almost blind in one eye and has a missing big toe.

Hawkins, who looks after the horses and our awkward goat, Gulliver, brought him to us.

"Perhaps you can change his mind, Madam," he said to Mimi. "He says he's going to work in one of they factories where they make ammunition. Dangerous work, I call it." He glared at Troggs. "Especially with only one good eye."

I don't think Mimi has ever laid eyes on Troggs. The nearest she goes to a horse is when she takes our pony and trap into town. She had a fall when she was young and hurt her right hand so badly that it's never been the same since. That's why she doesn't play the piano, or embroider or anything. But it turned out to be a blessing, because while it was healing, she tried writing and drawing with her left hand. Her writing was a mess, but as she worked more and more at her art, she discovered she has an amazing talent.

Some of our friends draw and paint, too, but their work is small, delicate and finely detailed. Mimi's paintings are large and colourful, with big, bold brush strokes. People can't understand why she works the way she does. "So unladylike," Elizabeth Baguley's mother said. But lots of people, especially Americans, want to buy her work. Papa used to take it all to a London gallery, where they sell it.

Gosh, that's something we'll have to do ourselves now.

Anyway, Troggs was not to be shifted. His family, it seems, has a history of soldiering and, while he cannot uphold that tradition, he can, he said, do something to help fight the Germans. Well, what he actually said was, "If they'm all brave enough to go fighting, Miss Daphne, then I ain't gonna be shirkin' me dooty." Something like that.

Mimi looked at me, shrugged and turned to Hawkins. "We must all be driven by our consciences."

He pressed his lips together, then said, "Well, I better be off and see to Gulliver, Madam. Goats won't wait for us to sort out our consciences. Come on, Troggs."

Though I'm sure he didn't mean to be impertinent, I'm quite sure Hawkins wouldn't have spoken like that in front of Papa.

1st February

I had a glorious ride on Honeycomb early this morning. As I passed the village, I met Elizabeth Baguley and her cousin, Reggie. They were riding out from Elizabeth's home, Great Oaks. Reggie's practically always there. His family live in London, but he loves to hunt and shoot and everything, so he often visits. Elizabeth has a pretty new bay mare. She's called Foxglove and has the gentlest temperament, just like her mistress! I always feel distinctly gawky next to Elizabeth. I know her mother thinks so, too. Probably another reason why I'm not invited to Great Oaks as often as I might be.

We rode together for a while and talked about Papa. They were both most kind. Then Reggie talked about the war, and how so many of his friends have either become cavalrymen or are planning to. How wonderful they must look in their uniforms, with shining spurs and swords flashing in the sun! Do they use swords these days, I wonder? Perhaps they just have guns. That's certainly not as romantic. I'm quite sure Reggie would be at war himself if he did not limp. He has one leg considerably shorter than the other.

We rode and talked for so long that breakfast had been cleared away by the time I reached home. I did what I always used to do as a child and visited the kitchen. I don't know that I'm as welcome now as I was when I was young, but I was too hungry to care.

"Here you are, Miss Daphne," said Mrs Rose. "Fresh from the oven." She handed me a hot bread roll, nestling in a white cloth, then set out a knife and dish of butter. Mmmm!

"Miss Daphne?"

"Yes, Mrs Rose?"

"Is your mother quite well?"

"She was when I left her after dinner last evening," I said. "We played a hand or two of cards and then retired for the night. Why?"

Mrs Rose busied herself with flour, eggs and sugar. "Oh, nothing, Miss. I just wanted to be sure she's all right. You know, with the master gone and everything."

How sweet.

2nd February

Just as I feel I'm coping with the loss of my darling Papa, somebody mentions him unexpectedly, or I look at his empty chair. It's as if someone has slammed a fist into my heart.

3rd February

The day got off to a rotten start. Honeycomb cast a shoe after less than a mile this morning, so I felt obliged to walk her back. Hawkins took care of her, but I was cross because I wanted some new gloves from the haberdasher's. I'm going to tea at Great Oaks tomorrow, and Elizabeth always looks so perfectly turned out.

I thought I'd have to wait for the pony and trap to be made ready, but Hawkins had a clever idea. "Why not take your bicycle out, Miss Daphne?" he suggested. "Lots of people have taken to bicycling since the war began."

And so I did! I haven't bicycled since Archie's last summer

holiday, when we went for a picnic with some bicycle-crazed friends. I was a little wobbly to start with today, and had trouble controlling my skirt, but was soon well away. I must admit I felt a little guilty, though. Papa would have been horrified to see me bicycling through the village streets! Not ladylike! Fortunately, no one of consequence saw me.

Afterwards, I went up to the studio to see Mimi, who was dappled with paint, as usual. She broke off from her work and sat down heavily in her basket chair. She looked rather "down in the dumps", as Elsie would say.

I told her of my trip to the haberdasher's. She said she envied me.

"Then you must come bicycling, too," I said. "On Monday! It will do you good – put some roses in your cheeks." (Strange. That's the sort of thing Mimi used to say to me. Now it's the other way around.) I laughed. "Just don't tell Uncle Cecil when you write!"

She sat up straight, looking appalled.

"Goodness!" she said. "I haven't written to him for days. How awful of me, Daffy. I must do so at once. He thinks he's found us an estate manager." She fetched pen and ink and paper.

Honestly! Fancy forgetting something as important as that! She's as bad as I am with my diary, although I write more regularly now.

As I left her to her letter, she gazed into the distance and said, "Now what was I going to say?"

"The *estate* manager," I reminded her. "And do *not* mention bicycles!"

5th February

I felt most uncomfortable yesterday. Bicycling uses different parts of the body from horse-riding, and I felt quite achy and bruised. Thankfully, Mimi completely forgot about coming bicycling with me.

Honeycomb is freshly shod, and Hawkins had groomed her until she shone. It was good of him to spend so much time on her, as he has much more work to do now Troggs has gone.

My visit to Elizabeth today was pleasant. She showed me her embroidery and her scrapbooks. I find them quite dull, but I was conscious that her mother is critical of me, so I spent a lot of time admiring them. We drank tea and ate bread and butter and tiny cakes. I ate far too many of those, but everyone was polite and said they'd really had enough, thank you, when I apologized. I'm not good at polite conversation, but I did make an effort.

"I cannot wait for high summer so we may have cucumber sandwiches again, Lady Baguley," I said. "Although your sandwiches are delicious," I added hastily.

"Thank you, Daphne," she replied. Icily, I thought.

Reggie offered to show me the crocus lawn. I thought that strange, as I've seen it many times before, as he well knows. However, Elizabeth whispered that it would be only polite to go with him, so I did. He's very friendly.

At dinner tonight, I told Mimi about my day and she said, "Reggie is a pleasant young man." Then she thought a bit and said, "I'm pleased that you visited Elizabeth. It's not good for you to stay home all the time. You scarcely leave the grounds these days."

"Mimi!" I said. "I'm always out and about on Honeycomb – or even bicycling!"

"Yes," she said, "but you're always alone."

That annoyed me a little, for if anyone spends all her time on her own, it's Mimi. When Archie's not around, I like my own company. And there's Honeycomb and Billie and all the other animals. I'm never alone.

Anyway, the other girls my age don't really like the sort of things I do. Whenever I'm with them I feel sort of – well, *squashed* is the only way I can explain it. It's like I want to burst free of them. I expect they feel the same about me.

7th February

A bright sunny day, almost like spring. I wrote some letters, took Billie for a stroll round the lake, then chatted to Mimi. She was concentrating on mixing some difficult shade of blue and wasn't really paying attention, so I took a book outside to find a sunny, sheltered corner. Then I saw the mulberry tree. Archie and I used to hide up there from Freddie, and I thought it would be nice to sit among the branches and read for a while. However, when I heard a motor car coming, I jumped down without thinking, and caught my skirt. It has a four-inch tear in it.

It's pointless giving it to Elsie to mend. She thinks her sewing is neat, but personally, I think she needs spectacles. She mended my lavender petticoat with white thread and then got blood on it from her pricked fingers. The result looked rather like Freddie's knee when the poor boy had it stitched.

So I took it to Mrs Hallibert, who wasn't in a very good mood. Mimi has friends for lunch (that was who was in the motor car) and Mrs Rose hadn't been able to get her to decide what to serve them. She'd grumbled to Mrs Hallibert who now grumbled to me.

"I suppose, with Madam the way she is, it'll be *me* who has to make these decisions," Mrs Hallibert muttered.

"What do you mean 'the way she is'?" I asked abruptly.

She hesitated. "Sorry, Miss Daphne. It's just me, wittering on to myself."

"But what did you *mean*?" I persisted.

She lifted the lid of her sewing basket. "Your mother's fine, Miss. Just busy, that's all, spends all her time in that studio. But it's nothing for you to worry your pretty head about."

9th February

Poor Hawkins asked if Mimi's done anything about getting a new stable lad.

"I can't carry on doing everything myself, Miss Daphne," he said. "That young village lad who's been helping out – well, he's willing, but not awful strong. He had a difference of opinion with Gulliver 'smorning and ended up on his back in the muck heap, if you'll pardon my language, Miss. He don't get on with goats."

I asked Mimi if Uncle Cecil had settled anything about the estate manager.

"Daffy darling," she said, glancing at her writing desk. "I ... oh dear..."

She obviously hadn't sent that letter to Uncle Cecil. But she looked so agitated I said, "Don't worry, I'll deal with it. You carry on with your painting." I glanced at it. "Heavens, is that a—" I looked closer. "It is! It's a fairy!"

"Yes," said Mimi, looking more relaxed. "Isn't she sweet? Her name's Lalu."

I laughed and left. Mimi might have relaxed, but I hadn't. How on earth do you go about getting a new stable lad? I imagine most young men are joining the army and wouldn't want to work on the estate.

10th February

I don't know why I worried. When I fetched Honeycomb this morning, I asked Hawkins if *he* knew what I should do.

"Bless you, Miss Daphne, if you'll just give me permission, I'll find us a new lad," he said as he altered my left stirrup. "Your father – God rest his soul – would have trusted me to do that, and your grandfather before him, God rest his soul, an' all."

He opened the yard gate and scratched Honeycomb's neck as we set off. "No, Miss Daphne, don't you worry your pretty little head about that."

I do wish people wouldn't keep saying that. Pretty little head indeed. It sounds as if my head's full of butterflies instead of brains.

13th February

Archie will be home tomorrow. Oh, it will be so good to have him back and not be lonely. What am I saying? I'm never lonely.

Well, sometimes I do feel a little alone, but that's not the same thing. There are Freddie and May, but they're always busy having lessons, or going for walks or visiting friends. And Mimi's usually busy with her work.

Speaking of Mimi, I took her a posy of snowdrops a couple of days ago. She loves them, and sometimes puts them in her paintings (they never turn out *quite* like the real thing). I looked at her latest work.

"That's the one I saw the other day, isn't it? You're slowing down!" I laughed.

"Heavens, no, darling," she said. "It's a different one."

I looked closer. "But there's the fairy. Lalu, you called her."

Mimi looked puzzled. "That's not Lalu, darling. It's Polan. He's Lalu's brother." She glanced back at the painting, head on one side. "Yes, I can see how you'd make that mistake. They are rather alike."

I felt quite disturbed as I left. Why is Mimi painting fairies, of all things? Her paintings are usually so powerful and vibrant. She's hardly a fairy sort of person.

But today I don't feel disturbed at all. Archie will be back in the morning. We can go riding together, and his friends will visit and spring's coming and we'll play cricket, and fish in the river – and I won't need to bother about whether other girls like my company or not. Everything will be just as it was before! Except for the war, of course.

Maybe Mimi's anxious because Freddie must soon go away to school.

14th February

Mimi put in an appearance just before ten this morning, dressed for receiving visitors. She wore a pretty hat, which she'd trimmed herself with an assortment of tiny feathers.

"I found them in the woods this morning," she said.

Odd. I hadn't seen her go out. It must have been very early.

I'm so excited at the thought of seeing Archie. Freddie's

beside himself, so Mimi asked Miss Rowan to take him and May for a brisk walk.

When they'd gone, the most awful thing happened. Mimi burst into tears! I gave her my handkerchief – she only ever has painty ones in her pocket – and put my arms round her.

"What is it, Mimi dear?"

She couldn't speak. Her sobs eventually subsided into sniffles. Her nose was running, so I looked away for a moment while she set herself straight. Then we sat together on a sofa beneath the open window while she composed herself.

"Please tell me what's wrong?" I begged.

Tears welled again and she shook her head.

"No, no," I said, "you must tell me. How can I help if I don't know what's wrong?"

She nodded, her mouth turned down at the corners, and fresh tears welled up. "Your father went away and never came home. He's not here, and it feels all wrong."

I might have mentioned that all over the country there were thousands of women whose husbands weren't there. Women whose husbands had gone into the greatest danger to serve their country, and who would never return. But I didn't. It wouldn't have helped.

"The estate manager starts on Monday," I said, trying to be practical, although I always feel tearful when she starts. "That means we'll no longer have to worry about making decisions.

25

Uncle Cecil has even agreed to go over the accounts every year." I hugged her. "All will be well."

Mimi shook her head. "It won't. Oh, Daffy, haven't you realized? Archie will soon be eighteen. He'll have to join the army. He'll go to France or Belgium and – and *fight*! Oh, it's driving me *mad* with worry!"

My heart plummeted into my boots. My brother – out there, on that awful front line thing. Germans, shooting at him, trying to kill him. Oh, I cannot bear it.

For Mimi's sake I tried so hard, but my own eyes filled. Please God, make this awful war stop. Come home, Archie.

16th February

Archie's back! He's grown so tall – at least three inches since the funeral, I swear! He no longer looks like a boy, but like a young man. Handsome, too! He shaves practically every day now, he tells me. I'm so happy.

The first thing he did, after being hugged to pieces by Mimi and me, and after being cooed at by Mrs Hallibert and Mrs Rose, was to go down to the stables to see the horses. Of course, I went, too.

The new lad was mucking out Gulliver's little stable. Archie didn't notice that the goat was loose and had spotted him. He strode straight to the paddock gate to call his horse, Firebrand.

"Look out!" I cried, as Gulliver gathered speed.

Too late. Goat and Archie met with a thump. Archie was livid. "Look at my trousers – they're filthy," he yelled, though why he was telling that to Gulliver is a mystery to me.

But soon Archie and Firebrand were reunited, and he set off for a wild gallop around the park, whooping with joy.

When Miss Rowan returned from a second excursion to the village with Freddie and May, there were loud shrieks of delight. Archie leapt off Firebrand, shook hands with Freddie and ruffled his hair. He swooped down on May, swept her up and swung her round. When he put her down, she brushed imaginary dirt off her clothes and said, "You smell of goat." Little fusspot.

Oh, it's good to have Archie home.

17th February

Archie was cross at breakfast this morning, because Mrs Rose doesn't send up half the dishes she used to.

When he complained that the sideboard was practically bare, I told him that it was on Papa's instructions. There's always so much left over (especially kidneys – ugh) and we shouldn't be wasteful when there's a war on. "Many people aren't as lucky as us," I finished. "There are food shortages, you know." That's because the Germans keep attacking our ships to stop them bringing supplies into the country. But we shouldn't complain. Things are far worse for the French.

Archie said I've grown pompous, and that if people were starving they could have the kidneys if they wished, but he wanted kippers.

Freddie agreed, but May simply wrinkled her nose.

19th February

Today I suggested Archie and I might ride over to call on Elizabeth. I'd rather have gone fishing or something, but he doesn't seem to want to do that sort of thing these days.

"Actually," Archie said, "I'm off to London to see some friends. We're having dinner, and I'll stay over at Eaton Square."

"Oh, that will be such fun!" I said. We used to stay at our town house quite often when Papa was alive.

He hesitated, then said, "Actually, Daffers, we'll all be men, you know. It's not really suitable for, er, well – you. And," he added hastily, "someone must stay with Mimi."

So. I don't feel hurt. Not really. But it's not the homecoming I'd imagined.

And what makes him think he's a *man* already?

22nd February

Archie enjoyed his London visit, needless to say. He brought me back a posy of violets, which was really sweet of him, as he must have felt a bit of a clot sitting on the train with them!

Mimi's working on a painting which, as far as I can see, is just fairies and little else.

"Is that the rest of Lalu's family?" I asked, expecting her to be amused.

"Yes," she said, without smiling, "and some of her friends."

It's quite worrying, the way her painting style has changed. Mrs Hallibert, too, thinks there's something odd about Mimi, although she doesn't say it directly, of course. She just makes comments like, "Madam must be missing the master," and "Wartime is worrying for a mother, Miss Daphne."

We've always been safe here in the country. We've never even seen a German Zeppelin, although Aunt Leonora has, and she says it's the most terrifying thing she's ever witnessed. Huge! Like a whale in the sky! But they hardly see them now, because our brave men kept shooting them down. They burn spectacularly if you fire into the gas that makes them fly, I believe. I don't think a German plane has ever flown near us, so why it's so particularly worrying for Mimi, I don't know. Yes, food is occasionally scarce, as they report in the newspapers, but we have plenty here. We grow all the vegetables and fruit we need, and there are eggs, milk and meat from the farms.

I suppose Mrs Hallibert means Mimi's worrying about Archie going to war. I keep it to myself, but I worry enough for both of us, I'm sure.

Maybe the war will be over soon – how much longer can it go on, for goodness' sake?

25th February

Aunt Eloise is visiting. She's actually my great-aunt, but Great-Aunt Eloise is such a mouthful that we all generally call her Aunt. I'm keeping her company while Mimi works, so haven't really done much lately.

We took Aunt Eloise to church this morning, and introduced her to the vicar. She rather liked him, and you could see that he warmed to her. Everybody does.

We prayed for our country, and for all our fine soldiers. I was in the choir stalls and I squinted across at Mimi, sitting in the Rowntree pew beside Aunt Eloise. She was flushed. I knew she was thinking of Archie and how he might soon become one of those soldiers.

Afterwards Aunt Eloise asked how long I'd been in the choir.

"Ages," I said.

"Odd that they asked you to step down from the choir to take the collection plate round," she said.

It makes me smile. When I applied to join the choir, they were far too polite to tell me I'm not much of a singer. But while I take the collection plate round, they have a chance for a good sing without me drowning out the people next to me! I don't mind.

2nd March

I'm so excited. Archie's invited me to visit a friend of his, about twelve miles away.

"He's got a corking sister, so you'll have good company," he told me.

I can go with him this time, because Aunt Eloise will be with Mimi. And she has plans!

"I'll take your mother away from that repulsively grubby studio for a few hours each day," she told me. "Get some spring air into her lungs and roses in her cheeks."

Good luck, I thought.

4th March

Archie's friend, John Wetherby, is nice, but not awfully bright. I don't know what Archie sees in him. His usual friends are lively and funny. John is, to be truthful, a bit of a pudding.

However, his sister, Violet, is delightful. As they don't live too far away, Archie's invited them to stay with us next weekend. I look forward to seeing Violet again.

9th March

John and Violet are to arrive this afternoon. Mrs Hallibert is displeased because I wish Violet to have the pink bedroom, which is the best, and which Aunt Eloise vacated only this morning.

"The bed will still be warm, Miss Daphne," she grumbled, but I pretended not to hear and went to pick daffodil buds for Violet's dressing table.

Later

Once the Wetherbys had settled in, we took tea overlooking the lawn. I like Violet very much, although she seems nervous of Billie, and clutches Archie's arm whenever my dear dog is near. I told her he's the gentlest dog imaginable (and extremely intelligent), but she wasn't convinced. However, we were soon chatting over butterfly cakes as if we'd known each other for ever, but Archie interrupted and offered to show her the garden.

I'd have burst out laughing if it hadn't been a rude thing to do. Archie! Interested in the garden! On an afternoon when there's a chill wind nipping you round every corner! I don't know what's come over him. However, once they'd gone, I was left with the dreary John, whose main topic of conversation was his stamp collection.

Postage stamps are all very well and, I daresay, quite interesting *if you can see them,* but if you can't, they are deadly dull.

When the others returned, I suggested Archie should show John the horses. Neither seemed keen, but I insisted. It was a way of getting my own back on Archie for leaving me with John.

As they left, Archie said, "Get Violet to tell you about

the things she's doing to help our soldiers win the war." He smiled at her. "She's amazing."

Well, I don't know why Archie thinks Violet is so amazing. All she's done is start a knitting group in their village hall. They knit socks and scarves and so on, for the troops in the trenches. Apparently, the poor men live a wet, freezing cold, muddy existence. Horrible.

As soon as the Wetherbys leave, I shall start something similar in our village hall. I'm as good as Violet, and I'll prove it to Archie.

Actually Violet and I could become friends if she'd get over her fear of Billie.

12th March

I *wondered* what Archie saw in John! Now I know. It's Violet! He really likes her. In fact I think he cares for her, a lot. They've spent much time together, and Archie even came with us when Violet and I picked catkins for Mimi.

And all that grabbing of Archie's arm when Billie was near was just so much twaddle. Violet's no more afraid of dogs than I am!

Archie's very downcast now they've left. Still, that's not my fault, and I have work to do. War work! Tomorrow morning, I'll go to the village hall and put up a notice inviting all women and girls to join my knitting group. It'll be called "Wool for War"! I'll be the organizer, and will pack up all the lovely knitted things and send them to our fighting men in France. Or Belgium, or wherever they are.

Mimi has promised to decorate my notice with pictures of socks and scarves and woollen hats and shivering soldiers. I hope she doesn't sneak in a fairy or two. They're in all her paintings now. Archie says she's going peculiar because of Papa's death. I didn't like to tell him that if she's going peculiar it's most likely because he, Archie, will soon go to war.

I asked if he'd thought about the future, and he has. A good deal. I was surprised and asked why he'd said nothing.

"War is men's business, Daffers," he said. "I'm not likely to bother you or Mimi about it, am I?"

At least he didn't mention my "pretty little head".

Later
Now I've realized why Archie brought me violets from London! They're obviously his favourite flowers now.

13th March

Oh, I am *mortified*! I went to the village hall this morning. I'd just pulled a chair to the wall, to stand on, when I heard footsteps behind me and, "Good morning, Miss Rowntree. We don't often see you in here."

I stepped down, my notice in hand, and turned to see Mrs Effingham-Jones, who does a huge amount for the village – she's always to be seen behind a stall at a sale of work or a bazaar. She's married to a retired army officer and likes to get out as much as she can.

I was just telling her she was the very person I wanted to see, when a group of women trooped in. Each carried a pretty floral bag.

"Ah," I said, "how fortunate. I'm Daphne Rowntree..."

"Yes, Miss, we know," said one, "Miss Rowntree from the big house."

I smiled. "I've had such a good idea. I'd like to invite you all to join 'Wool for War'!"

Blank faces.

"My knitting group!" I said brightly. "To knit comforts for soldiers!"

One or two glanced at each other; the rest looked down at their feet. Then Mrs Effingham-Jones said, not unkindly, "We are already a knitting group, Miss Rowntree," and, to my horror, they *all* reached into their floral bags and pulled out an assortment of half-knitted woollen things.

They invited me to join their group. I wasn't sure how to reply. I didn't want them to feel uncomfortable because of my presence, but it seemed rude to refuse – it *is* a war effort. In the end, Mrs Effingham-Jones pulled a chair forward and said, "Do sit here, Miss Rowntree." In no time I was part of their circle, feeling most awkward and clutching a ball of wool and some needles.

My governess tried to teach me to knit when I was small, but I was never good at it, and I haven't improved with age. I keep forgetting to put the wool round to the other side and end up with far too many stitches. The women helped when I asked, but I'm sure they considered me an utter fool. Of course they'd all thought of knitting for soldiers before me. Silly Miss Rowntree from the big house, coming down to organize their lives, when they're all far more capable than me.

In the end, they took away my needles and gave me a skein of wool to hold while someone else wound it into a ball.

I felt totally out of my depth.

22nd March

Uncle Cecil's here for the night so he can have talks with the new estate manager, who is proving to be a real boon. That's quite funny, because his name is actually Mr Boone! Uncle Cecil's also removed another anxiety from me. He's going to deliver Mimi's latest batch of paintings to the gallery in London.

He arrived in a new glossy black motor car. It's been given to him by the government. Well, it's not a gift, exactly, it's for him to use while he's working for them. After he'd seen to estate matters, Uncle Cecil sent Elsie to fetch Archie to Papa's study.

I asked Elsie what it was about, and she didn't know, so we stayed on the stairs. When the study door opened, I pretended to be asking her about some lost lace. Archie winked at me and jerked his head towards the front entrance. I followed him outside and caught up as he strode along the front of the house.

"What is it?" I asked.

He was bursting with excitement. "Uncle Cecil remembered Papa's motor car," he said. "It's lying idle, and Boone is to teach me to drive!"

How utterly thrilling! My little brother, driving a motor car!

23rd March

Before he left this morning Uncle Cecil spent a couple of hours with Mimi in Papa's study. When they emerged, her eyes were pink-rimmed. She must be desperate for her brother to stay, but he has Aunt Leonora and my cousin Roberta to look after – and his government work, of course.

My uncle kissed her cheek and led her to the morning room. Then he came back to me and we walked outside where his motor car was waiting. It was drizzling, so I stayed beneath the portico. I assumed that Mimi's paintings were carefully wrapped and stowed away in the back of the car.

"Daffy, keep an eye on your mother, won't you?"

"Of course," I said. "Uncle Cecil, did you look at her latest pictures? There are lots of—"

"Fairies, I know," he said. "Most odd. Not herself at all." He patted Billie's head. "One thing's for certain, Daffy. I won't be taking those to the gallery! Who'd buy them?"

He kissed me and squeezed my hand, then looked round. "Where's Archie?"

Honk! Honk!

"There!" I pointed along the drive. Coming slowly towards us, with a lot of wheel-wobbling, was Archie – in Papa's motor car! He was already driving it!

Oh, it does look fun!

26th March

Mrs Effingham-Jones called today. The maid showed her into the small sitting room and I ordered tea.

We discussed the fine weather and the knitting group. I haven't returned to it, but I have purchased fresh skeins of wool for Elsie to take to them. (Elsie asked if she might join them for an hour on Tuesday mornings, and I was glad to give her permission.)

Eventually tea arrived, with some delicious little sugar biscuits, and Mrs Effingham-Jones got round to what she wanted to discuss.

"Miss Rowntree," she began, "I know you wanted to be part of a – um – our knitting group, but you, er, well—"

I helped her. "I'm not a natural knitter, Mrs Effingham-Jones."

"Quite," she said. "But we have a new group that meets on Wednesdays, and we wondered – since you're keen to do war work – if you'd like to join us. Of course," she added hurriedly, "in normal circumstances, we wouldn't dream of asking *you* to come to the village hall, but – well – there *is* a war on, and every little helps."

She's a very nice woman. "I understand perfectly, Mrs Effingham-Jones," I said. "I'd be delighted to help. I hope it's a task I can manage!"

"Oh yes!" she said. "We roll bandages!"

Roll bandages. Well, people obviously think that even Miss Rowntree can roll a bandage.

28th March

I'm a horrible, small-minded person. I went to bandage-rolling at the village hall, feeling slightly grumpy and prepared to be bored rigid, but I wasn't! It was fun! We had tea and biscuits, and everybody talked. Actually, there wasn't much chatter at first – people were rather stiff, and I noticed lots of glances in my direction. But just as I finished rolling my first bandage, I dropped it and it unrolled down the length of the hall. Without thinking I said, "Damn!"

Everybody looked slightly shocked, and I know I went red. Then I started to giggle and said, "Sorry. My brother says it all the time, and it sort of rubs off after a while." They laughed. I think they were more surprised than shocked. I'm sure their men folk use bad language occasionally. They just didn't expect it from "Miss Rowntree from the big house".

After that, we got on swimmingly, and I learned all about their husbands – good and bad – and their children. I'm looking forward to next Wednesday. At last I'm doing something towards the war, even though it's not very much.

Later

I took Honeycomb out for a gallop this afternoon. It was the most glorious day. Sunshine, a stiff breeze, puffy white clouds chuffing across the sky, and yellow primroses dotting the hedgerows. Splendid!

As we ambled back across the park, I heard the growl of a motor. Of course it was Archie. I tied Honeycomb up to a tree, away from the racket he was making, and went to see.

He drove round in circles, showing off like mad. I don't think he quite has the hang of steering, as he jerks from side to side rather a lot.

"Fancy a spin, Daffers?" he asked.

"No, thanks," I said. "I'll wait till you're a little more competent."

He stuck his tongue out and drove off. He hasn't grown up all that much!

I envy Archie. It must be wonderful to sit behind that

steering wheel and make the motor car do exactly as you want. A bit like riding Honeycomb, I suppose, only noisier.

I'd love to have a go!

1st April

Archie has more friends than he knew! They all want to have a go at driving. Most of them aren't very good, but I've noticed that they're the ones who jump in and try to drive without listening to what Archie has to say. Those who listen, learn.

Mimi's still putting fairies in her pictures. They all have names, too. It's as if she knows them personally! Tiny Lalu has a huge family and dozens of friends – old ones, young ones, even babies!

3rd April

Two of Archie's friends – the better drivers – spent all afternoon with him and the motor car. When they'd gone, I asked if I could have a go.

"You!" he said, as if I'd told him I planned to grow a beard.

"Why not?" I asked. "You know I'm a much better rider than most of your friends, and I can ride a bicycle, too. Why shouldn't I have a go at driving?"

He was highly amused at this but opened the door for me. Then he went around the front with the starting handle, stuck it in a hole somewhere and swung it round and round until the motor started.

Oh, how can I put into words the thrill I got when I actually made the car move for the first time? I MUST learn to drive!

8th April

Easter Sunday, and the church was full of spring flowers. What a joyous service! I sang my heart out! I know people could see I was enjoying it, because many of them kept glancing my way.

I was amused to discover there'd been a choir practice on Thursday morning and nobody told me about it! Never mind. I know all the hymns backwards.

The Americans have declared war on Germany. How strange that we're pleased about that, just as we're celebrating Easter.

10th April

I am so proud of myself. Even Archie says I'm a naturally good driver, and have a feel for machinery! I am, frankly, a better driver than he is. And being behind the steering wheel makes me feel so sophisticated and glamorous!

11th April

Honeycomb and I were trotting towards the village today, when I saw the Baguley ladies riding towards me, with Reggie alongside. We stopped to speak.

"And where are you off to, Daphne?" asked Lady Baguley. "To the hall, perhaps, to spend time with the village women?"

I know I went red, but it was not embarrassment. It was anger. That woman can be so offensive!

"Yes, Lady Baguley," I replied politely. "We do war work."

Reggie grinned. "I say, Miss Rowntree, do you really?"

Elizabeth smiled, too. "Bandage-rolling, isn't it, Daphne?"

Cat!

I gave Reggie my biggest smile. I think he's the only person I know who doesn't think me odd.

We parted, but a moment or two later, I heard hooves pounding, and turned to see Reggie cantering towards me.

"I say, Miss Rowntree, I think it's marvellous that you're so patriotic."

"Thank you," I said.

"Er, how is your brother, er, Archibald?" he asked. "Must ride over to see him sometime."

"Do," I said. "He'll be delighted. Good day, Reggie."

At lunch, I told Mimi and Archie about my encounter with the Baguleys. Mimi was more interested in Reggie.

"It will be pleasant if he calls on Archie," she said.

Archie grunted. "Don't even remember what he looks like. Can't imagine why he's keen to call on me."

Mimi said, "Perhaps it's not you he's keen to see."

I looked up, wondering what on earth she meant. She was concentrating on her plate, but glanced up with the most innocent look on her face.

Archie absolutely honked with laughter when he saw my expression. "He's coming to see you, you ninny! He has a fancy for you!"

Oh, heavens, I thought. That won't please the Baguleys.

Mimi changed the subject. "I want you to go to the London gallery in a week or two, Daffy darling," she said.

"Speak to the owner and find out if he likes my new paintings."

"But I thought—"

Ignoring me, she continued, "Your uncle Cecil wouldn't take them, so I've sent them myself, by carrier. There's absolutely no need to mention this to him."

Gosh.

"Archie often goes to London," I said. "Couldn't he do it?"

Again, Mimi continued as if I hadn't spoken. "You're going to visit your cousin Roberta," she said. "Cecil and Leonora have invited you."

"Oh, I see." I haven't seen Roberta for ages. We don't visit London much, not now the war's on. I remember her as being very brainy and dull. She didn't want to ride or swim or anything when we were younger.

"But that will leave just you and Archie at home," I protested. "Let Archie go. I don't really want to."

"They'd like you to."

Archie looked at Mimi and seemed about to say something. She stared at her tomato salad.

He cleared his throat. "The thing is, Daffers, old girl, I'm joining up. I'm eighteen now, and I'm off to the war. Me and Firebrand." He grinned. "You can have the car to yourself."

12th April

I've argued all I can. Archie will join the cavalry, and that's that. He would have to join something, because it's the law.

I refused to go to London and leave Mimi alone, but she's thought of that. Aunt Eloise is coming to stay – for several months. She no longer wishes to be at her Essex home, because it's dangerous on the coast, she says. German aeroplanes – Gothas – fly over to drop bombs.

Aunt Eloise is probably the best person to be here. I'm actually quite worried about Mimi. This morning I picked the last of our hyacinths for her dressing table. She breathed in the scent, then said, "Lovely, Daffy darling! These are Lalu's favourite colour."

I didn't tell Archie – he's too busy getting ready to leave. Should I tell Uncle Cecil? I don't know. Perhaps Mimi was joking.

Aunt Eloise will sort her out.

18th April

Archie left today. When we said goodbye I buried my face in Firebrand's warm neck for comfort. Archie patted both me and Billie.

21st April

I've been so miserable. Mimi spends a lot of time wandering round the woods now. I must say, she always looks happier when she returns, clutching a posy of wild flowers or leaves. But she's so strange these days.

23rd April

Aunt Eloise arrived, grumbling because her train was late. It was worse for me, because I'd accompanied Hawkins to the station, and had nothing to do but wander the hedgerows until she appeared. I found some lovely crab-apple blossom for Mimi, though, so the time wasn't entirely wasted.

I had a brief chat with Aunt Eloise before she met Mimi, and told her my worries. "There's nothing I can put my finger on," I said. "She just seems, well, strange."

Aunt Eloise was understanding. "Anxiety affects people in different ways," she said, clasping my hands between her own. "Some people retreat into their own imaginations, where it feels safe. Is she painting still?"

"Oh yes," I said. "Beautiful work – much softer than usual, but full of fairies. And oh, Aunt Eloise, she's sent some to the gallery – nothing like the ones they're used to receiving. She's asked me to go and see what's happening to them. Suppose the gallery people refuse to sell them? Mimi would be broken-hearted."

"Hush now," said Aunt Eloise. "If they refuse them, we won't tell her. It's as simple as that. She has no communication herself with the gallery, so it will be easy to deceive her. Knowing your mother, I'm quite sure she never checks where her money comes from or how much she has, so that's not a problem."

I feel so much better now my aunt is here. And she's agreed to help Mimi and me run the household. "Help" is not the right word! I think Aunt Eloise will be shocked to see how little my mother does, and how poorly I do the rest. I rely heavily on Mrs Hallibert's experience.

25th April

At bandage-rolling today, I noticed that three of the youngest women were missing.

"They've gone to work in the factory, down the valley," I was told. It seemed odd to me. Why would girls – for they were little more than that – want to make tools or nails or whatever they produce down there?

I soon found out. The factory's been changed and now it makes munitions, whatever they are – things to do with the war. How exciting!

26th April

I looked up "munitions" in the dictionary this morning. It means weapons or ammunition. It must feel wonderful to make something that a soldier will actually use to fight for his country!

After tea I drove round the park in the motor car. It's such fun! Then I called Billie and took Honeycomb for a gentle canter. We went to the highest point beyond our land and looked across the valley. I could see the factory.

Aunt Eloise took Mimi out today to call on friends. "Your mother hasn't left the estate for a while," she told me. "It's done her good. I just hope she doesn't expect me, in return, to listen to her talk about her little fairy characters!"

Aunt Eloise is quite fun.

27th April

A postcard from Archie arrived today. He's still training, and has had a photograph taken of himself in his uniform, with Firebrand. How grand! I can't wait to see it.

29th April

Uncle Cecil's here again. I told him I can drive. He was quite impressed, and let me take him for a spin. He wanted to go up to the crossroads and back, but I told him I tend to stay on the estate lanes because I don't think my friends' mothers would approve of me driving. So we went down to the river and back.

Uncle Cecil seems tired, and Mimi hardly spoke at dinner, so I did all the talking. I mentioned my war work. That made him sit up!

"What are you talking about?" he demanded.

Mimi put a hand on his arm. "It's nothing dreadful, Cecil."

"Not at all," said Aunt Eloise. "Tell him, Daffy."

I skipped over the knitting fiasco, then told him about bandage-rolling. I mentioned that some of the village girls work in the munitions factory.

"Good for them," he said.

I was so taken aback by his reaction that I spoke without thinking. "I should like to do that sort of war work, too."

He froze with his fork stuck in his lamb cutlet. "Are you out of your mind? Your place is here, with your mother. You're all she has at home now."

"But there's Aunt Eloise, and I do so want to do some—"

"It's not what you want," he snapped. "It's what's right and proper. Young ladies of your station do not work in factories. Most unseemly. Your father would turn in his grave – begging your pardon, ladies. Your task in life is to learn to run a home so that you can support whatever man is fool enough to marry you."

That was unkind and I had to look down because my eyes filled. He seems to be putting himself in a father's place now I don't have my Papa.

Afterwards, we sat in the drawing room. Mimi did a pencil sketch for a new painting and Uncle Cecil read. When Aunt Eloise took up her tapestry, I dug out some embroidery I keep neglecting. Pale pink flowers on a dove-grey sash, with red specks where my pricked fingers have bled on to the silks.

Uncle Cecil may be right, but it does seem a shame. I won't learn much about running a home from someone who paints fairies. I'd be far better off doing war work of some sort. Thousands of women do. Why not me? I'm no use at anything else, apart from driving and riding and things like that. I'm not like Elizabeth Baguley – the domestic life is just not right for me. Or rather, I'm not right for it. So what am I right for?

Later
I'm livid about Uncle Cecil's reaction, and I told Archie so when I wrote to him. He'll understand.

30th April

Before he left, Uncle Cecil took me aside.

"I was a little harsh last night," he said, "but I must consider your upbringing carefully now your father is gone. Your mother is ... not herself. I still stand by what I said – you cannot and will not work in a factory – but there is other war work you can do."

"Really?"

"Join some sort of organization," he said. "An organization that's especially for young ladies like you. You can't run around with village girls. That's not where you belong."

I felt like saying that I didn't think I belonged anywhere, but I was curious to know what he meant. "What sort of organization?"

"I don't know," he said. "Your Aunt Leonora's got herself involved with something. Keeps her occupied, and she says they're a fine bunch of women. I'd mention it to her but I'm going away for a couple of weeks. Drop her a line. She'll steer you in the proper direction."

I'll do better than that. As I have to go and stay with Roberta, I can speak to her mother in person!

2nd May

A letter from Archie arrived in the evening post. I hate him. He says he absolutely agrees with Uncle Cecil that I shouldn't do war work.

Well, things have changed since I wrote that letter. And of course I don't really hate him. I'm just annoyed with him for not standing up for me. And I'm angry because he's crossing the Channel today. Not only that, but John and Violet Wetherby were going to see him off. I'd like to have done that. I almost think he prefers Violet to me.

3rd May

It's just sunk in and I feel so miserable. How could I have thought cross thoughts about Archie? My brother's gone to war, and it's bound to be dangerous.

5th May

I'm going to visit Roberta tomorrow. Aunt Eloise said it will do me good, and I mustn't worry about Mimi.

That made me feel mean, because I've actually been worrying about Archie, rather than my mother. Also, I'm sorry for myself because, after Mimi telling me for years that when I grow up I can do anything I want, and be anything I want, it seems I can't.

I'm tired of sorting out menus with Mrs Rose, and doing domestic tasks and embroidering that wretched sash (which I seem to have been doing for years). Not to mention bandage-rolling, which may be worthy but is just so tedious.

Women leave home every day to do important things. Even Mimi does something worthwhile. She paints pictures people pay good money for. Well, she did. Certainly no one in their right mind will want her fairies.

If others do things that matter, why can't I? The only task I have ahead of me is to visit the gallery. That will be somewhat embarrassing. I'll need to have the unsold pictures sent home, and must instruct the staff not to mention them to Mimi. We'll find somewhere to store them until her mind is stronger.

But there's still one ray of hope. I have Aunt Leonora's organization to investigate.

6th May

Gosh! Roberta's changed. She's not brainy and dull any more. Well, I'm sure she's still brainy, but she's certainly not dull. Everyone except Uncle Cecil – even Aunt Leonora – calls her Bobby, for short. And she has had her *hair* cut short – in a bob! It's rather stylish, but it is a little ... well, unfeminine, I suppose.

Bobby goes to lots of meetings about women's rights (I was beginning to think we didn't have any, after Uncle

Cecil's and Archie's pronouncements) and to meetings about women being allowed to vote. It all sounds rather intense to me.

When I said I wanted to do something in the war, she said, "Then you must jolly well do it, Daffers! We all should."

Easy for her to say.

Later

I've found out what Aunt Leonora's war work is. It's not very warlike. She works in an office in Earl's Court Road, in London, for an organization called the First Aid Nursing Yeomanry. Yeomanry! I looked it up in Uncle Cecil's dictionary, which says it's a volunteer cavalry force. The cavalry ride horses! (It also said yeomanry's for men, but I'm ignoring that as Aunt Leonora says the FANY are all women.)

And this is the organization Uncle Cecil recommended me to find out about. War work and horses! That's for me! Don't know about the "nursing" bit, though.

I didn't get to sleep until after the landing clock had struck four. Too much on my mind!

7th May

I'm completely dumbfounded!

I made Bobby go to the art gallery with me today. I didn't want to deal with the proprietor on my own.

"I'll feel stupid," I explained. "If you're there it won't be so bad."

"Oh, Daffers, you are wet," she said. "He's only a man. Why should he make you feel stupid?"

I explained about the fairies.

"Oh, I see," she said. "That's different. But your poor mama! She's just not coping, is she? Never mind. We'll tell the gallery owner that she has no end of people wanting to buy her fairy pictures, so she won't mind at all having these back."

When we met the proprietor, it seemed that my worst fears were about to be realized. After he'd greeted us, and offered refreshment, he said, "The situation's a little difficult. Mr Rowntree's style has changed. He's started painting..." He hesitated, so I took the opportunity to correct him.

"Excuse me," I said, "you mean *Mrs* Rowntree."

He stared. "But... Oh. Oh, I see."

I didn't see. "Sir," I said, "were you under the impression that these paintings were done by my father?"

"Well, yes," he said. "The signature, you know... It was just initials and he never said... How could I tell?"

Bobby spoke through tight lips. "So you assumed the artist must be a man? You didn't think a woman could possibly have painted something as good, and as saleable?"

"I'm sorry." The proprietor turned to me. "Your father never corrected me, Miss Rowntree."

I was too tired to care. "Never mind, sir. You were saying about the change of style. I assume you'd like to return the new pictures."

He shook his head violently. "Not at all! Oh, not at all! In fact, I've none to return. I sold them all to an American dealer."

"Goodness!" was all I could manage. Bobby's chin dropped.

"The difficulty I mentioned," the flustered man continued, "is that the dealer's American clients would like more of the pictures where fairies feature in a small way in woodland scenes, but not, I regret to say, the ones that are solely of fairies."

He shall have them. Mimi will be so pleased! And he's asked that she sign them with her full name.

"Somehow," he explained, "it seems more fitting that they come from the brush of a lady."

61

Bobby and I headed straight for the nearest hotel, to celebrate over a pot of tea and slices of very jammy Victoria sponge. (I wonder if the king will have a cake named after him, as the last queen did. Somehow "George sponge" sounds unappetizing!)

I'm going straight home tomorrow. I can't wait to give Mimi the good news!

8th May

I was so excited to be home and Mimi was as thrilled as I'd expected.

"Daffy, darling, that's wonderful!" she said. "Isn't it, Aunt Eloise?"

"Wonderful!"

I knew what my aunt was thinking. This was just the news Mimi needed to cheer her, to make her concentrate on real things.

Or so we thought. At dinner, Mimi refused pudding and said, "Please excuse me if I go to bed. It's been such an exciting evening, and I want to be up early to go and give the good news to Lalu and Polan."

She smiled happily as Aunt Eloise and I stared, dismayed.

"How thrilling," she went on as she left, "that they'll be known in America!"

I put my head on the table and sobbed. I hate crying in front of the servants, but that wasn't the worst of it. I got vanilla cream in my hair, and it was only washed two days ago.

9th May

I feel better today. After a long discussion with Aunt Eloise I realize that Mimi is happy with a head full of fairies. It's good, really, because it means she doesn't worry so much about Archie. If she didn't have her fairies, she'd be in tears all the time. I couldn't bear that.

I'll talk to her about me joining the FANY. That will give her something else to think about. Maybe it will take her mind off Lalu and Polan. Heavens! *I'm* talking about fairies now! Get a grip, Daffy!

10th May

Well, that went all right – in the end.

I explained to Mimi and Aunt Eloise about the FANY, and what Aunt Leonora does in the office in Earl's Court Road. Actually, I made that bit up, because I don't know exactly what work she does – all I'm interested in is that it's to help the war effort.

"So I should like to join the FANY," I finished.

Mimi picked at some blue paint under her nails. "Ooh, I don't know, Daffy darling," she said. "I'm not sure if it would suit you."

"Mimi, you always said I could do anything, be anything."

"But darling, I meant you could be a good tennis player, and row a boat, and ride a horse – and I was right. Why, you can even drive a car! How many young women can do that? But joining an ... organization..."

She made it sound like a weird club for people who aren't quite our sort.

"Please say I can," I begged. "Archie's fighting in the war, some of the village women are making munitions, and Papa gave his life for our country. I so want to do something, too. Please, Mimi. I must."

She turned to Aunt Eloise. "Daffy's certainly got a bee in her bonnet," she said. "What do you think?"

"I think you should say yes," said my wonderful aunt. "It will be good for Daffy. She has a need to do something and, to me, that's praiseworthy. Besides, how dangerous can it be, if Leonora belongs to it?"

Mimi shrugged. "Very well, Daffy darling."

I hugged them both and hurried to my room to write to Aunt Leonora.

12th May

Aunt Leonora has replied. She seems pleased, and says, "You're rather young to join the FANY, but we won't let that stop us, will we?"

I do have some terrific aunts.

13th May

A letter arrived at lunchtime from Uncle Cecil. Aunt Leonora has told him of my wish, and I have his blessing! But, he says, I may only be in the FANY for as long as Aunt Eloise stays with Mimi. And I must be careful and not get into dangerous situations.

Dangerous situations – in Earl's Court Road! The really dangerous place to be is at sea, it seems to me. There have been so many attacks on merchant ships by U-boats that the Navy is having to supply ships as escorts, to try to destroy the submarines.

15th May

I've wasted no time. I'm back at Bobby's, and tomorrow Aunt Leonora's taking me to the FANY office. Bobby can't come, as she has one of her give-women-rights meetings, and she won't miss that for anything.

16th May

Goodness! The FANY is like an army. They wear a smart uniform, and they're so efficient. The women who run the organization are very busy, but I suppose they would be, since they need to know where people are and where to send them, and what they must do when they get there. Some of the FANY are in Belgium and France; others are in England working hard to raise money and get new recruits. That's probably what I'll do to start with. I hope I get a chance to go to France. We used to go there for holidays before the war, and it's very lovely, with deliciously different food.

Speaking of food, the FANY women pay for their keep and so on, and supply their own uniforms. And they give a regular subscription to the organization itself.

I don't mind paying. It all helps the war effort, and I can afford it without asking Mimi. I have a good dress allowance – Elizabeth always says I have far more than she does. How, then, does she always manage to look so neat, when I don't?

But I will look neat in a uniform! I cannot wait to get it. It's sold in Gamage's, which is a large store made up of different departments. I've never been there, but I would adore to.

Anyway, during my interview, the Organizing Officer asked why I wanted to join the FANY, and I said it was because I wanted to do something useful, like my brother. They asked if I'd done anything else, so I told them I'd tried to organize the village women to do war work. It was sort of true – I did *try* to organize the knitting.

They said I came highly recommended as being of good character. Someone (thanks, Aunt Leonora) told them I'd never enter into any obligation I was unable to fulfil. That's a FANY way of saying I wouldn't join if I didn't think I could cope.

I have to do a first-aid course. I gulped at that, as I don't like blood. I'd been so thrilled at the word "yeomanry" when I first heard about the FANY that I'd completely forgotten the first-aid bit! Anyhow, Aunt Leonora promised I wouldn't be doing any nursing, so that's all right. I suppose you need to know first aid in case another FANY falls over, or cuts herself or something.

I was asked about my skills. Apart from being a fairly good bandage-roller, I couldn't think of anything. I'm sure they wouldn't be interested in my lumpy embroidery. I said that of course I can ride, and they nodded, and then I remembered...

"I can drive a motor car," I said.

Didn't that make them sit up! I wonder why. Perhaps I should find out a little more about the FANY. I'll ask Aunt Leonora tomorrow. They told me to do that, actually. A stern woman with badges, and stripes on her sleeves, said, "Miss Rowntree, thank you very much for coming and for your interest in the First Aid Nursing Yeomanry. May I suggest you have a proper discussion with Armstrong and make absolutely sure you want to join us."

For a moment I wondered who on earth Armstrong was, then I remembered. It's Uncle Cecil and Aunt Leonora's name!

I'm reasonably sure this is what I want to do, but tomorrow, first thing, I will have that discussion with Aunt Leonora. Oh, gosh! Will I soon have to call her Armstrong? How odd!

17th May

I started the proper discussion straight after breakfast. Aunt Leonora's contribution was simply to flap an arm in the air and say, "Don't worry about it, darling. You'll love it!" Then she dumped her napkin on the table, pushed her chair back and left the room.

Well, that's all right then.

23rd May

Aunt Eloise is so grateful, she says, to be staying with us. A whole load of German bombers attacked London on Wednesday. It was too dark for them to see much, so they dropped their bombs east of the city and killed about a hundred Canadian soldiers at a military base. Canada has been with us since the start of the war, and those poor souls were probably expecting to be sent to the front soon. They must have thought they were safe till then. How frightening, when the enemy might come at you across the land, from beneath the sea or from the sky.

1st June

Before the war, new recruits to the FANY went to a sort of camp. That sounds the most ripping fun! It was there that they did their first-aid course and learned to make their beds and to follow orders. But now there isn't time. My first-aid course took three afternoons, and I was taught by members of the British Red Cross Society.

It was quite straightforward and I sort of passed. There wasn't any blood or anything, but I felt quite queasy bandaging a collarbone. When you look in the mirror you can practically see your collarbone, and the thought of it breaking made me feel sick. And I didn't like the idea of hooking false teeth out of unconscious people's mouths. Ugh.

The instructor said she was thankful I wasn't thinking of going into nursing, but my bandaging was good and they felt I had common sense and would remain calm in a crisis. I'll say so. You should have seen how calm I was when Billie had a fight with a nasty vicious dog. I simply turned my back until they'd finished. To be truthful, I couldn't bear to look, but Billie was fine. He won. He always does.

Anyway, it's driving next. I'll show them!

8th June

Oh dear. My driving course hasn't gone *quite* as well as I'd expected. First of all, I had to start the wretched thing. I've never started a car before. Archie or Hawkins or someone always did it for me.

You stick the starting handle in a hole in the front of the motor car, then turn like mad, and that gets the engine going. It's jolly difficult. I don't know why they wanted me to do it, when there were so many mechanics standing around idle. Anyway, you turn and turn and eventually the car starts. Then you get in the driving seat and off you go.

Indeed, off I went. That was wrong, because I was supposed to wait for the instructor. He was a British Red Cross Society man and when he caught up, he was very stiff and starchy.

"Listen to me, Miss," he said. "I'm in charge here, and you do as I tell you. That's the rule, and it's to keep us all safe. D'you understand, Miss?"

I apologized, and was a perfect angel for the rest of the drive. I do think I surprised him with my ability, because the only orders he gave me after that were, "Not so fast, Miss," or "Not so close, Miss," or "Watch out, Miss."

Afterwards, he said I drove too fast ("It's not a race, Miss!") but I'm a jolly good driver for a woman, which really cheered me. I came away feeling cock-a-hoop.

13th June

I've finished my driving course, and took my test today. If I say so myself, I did jolly well, and passed with flying colours. The only words the tester spoke the whole time (apart from telling me which way to go and so forth) were, "I say, steady on, Miss."

I'm going home in the morning, then when the reports on my first-aid and driving courses come through, I'll go to Gamage's to buy my uniform, and become a real FANY. How thrilling this is!

14th June

Archie. My darling brother.

Oh, I never thought to know such misery and confusion. I was so happy and excited when I came home. I should have known something terrible had happened when Hawkins met me at the station and barely spoke. I assumed he was in

73

a foul mood because Gulliver had bitten him or butted him or something.

Mimi and Aunt Eloise were in the drawing room, both with swollen, red-rimmed eyes. Mrs Hallibert hovered with cups of tea and just looked at me, unable to speak, before leaving the room.

"What is it?" I cried as I knelt in front of my mother. "Mimi, what's happened? Are you ill?"

She shook her head. "Oh, Daffy darling, it's ... it's..." She kept gulping, and seemed unable to speak.

I turned to Aunt Eloise.

"Daffy dear," she said, "it's Archie, but you—"

I didn't hear any more, just a long wail, and the wail was coming from me. "No!" I leapt up. "No!"

"Daffy!" Aunt Eloise gripped my shoulders. "Pull yourself together, dear. It's not the worst."

I took a deep breath. "Not…? Not the worst?"

"No, dear. Archie is missing. That's all we know. Now, go to your mother, and I'll ring for more tea. We must be hopeful."

I looked down at Mimi. She rocked back and forth, hugging her knees. At first I thought she was humming, but she wasn't. It was just the sound of her agony.

15th June

Such dreadful news about another big attack on London – in daylight – by German bombers. Over a hundred poor souls dead, and hundreds more wounded. And the aeroplanes all got away.

So many people have to endure so much sadness.

I am doing my best to be hopeful about our own sadness. Archie will return. He's probably had a bump on the head and lost his memory and wandered off. Someone will find him, and he'll have something on him that will tell them who he is, and they'll look after him, and write to us to say he's safe. And then he'll come home. I know he will.

No I don't.

Later
Poor Freddie and May. Miss Rowan is doing her best to comfort them.

17th June

We are all doing our best. The children are having lessons as normal. The servants are going about their business as usual, but Elsie is being the most useless maid imaginable at the moment. She is upset, too, so I cannot get cross with her.

Mimi stayed in bed this morning, so I took Aunt Eloise out for a ride. She warned me that she's not a horsewoman, and she's right. Hawkins saddled our kindly old mare, and put her on a lead rein, which I held.

It was a pleasant, gentle ride, if slow, and we talked non-stop. Eventually, we got off the subject of poor Archie and were commenting on the various wild flowers we spotted. It was almost fun.

What poor Aunt Eloise must have thought when I suddenly cried out, "Firebrand!" I cannot imagine. I swung Honeycomb's head round and turned for home, urging her into a gallop. Mercifully, I dropped the lead rein, otherwise I should think poor Aunt Eloise would have gone flying. As it was, it was a relief that the old mare remembered her way home, since Aunt Eloise was too shaken to find it by herself.

I galloped into the yard and leapt off Honeycomb without

waiting for help. Hawkins came running out of the tack room. "Miss Daphne? What is it?"

"Firebrand," I sobbed. "My brother's horse must be missing, too."

Oh, the poor creature. Lost in France, or Belgium, or wherever they are. He must be so bewildered without someone to love him and take care of him.

Hawkins pressed his lips together for a moment before he spoke. "I like to believe, Miss Daphne, that wherever Mr Archie is, Firebrand is too."

Bless him. That was such a comfort. Of course they might be lost together. Oh, how I wish Firebrand could bring Archie home the way the old mare brought Aunt Eloise.

18th June

Violet Wetherby called today. Mimi asked her to stay for dinner and overnight. We were very informal this evening, as Violet hadn't brought anything to change into. She'll be gone in the morning, and I'm glad of that, as I only want to be with my family.

Violet, however, is reacting almost as if she were family. She's terribly distressed about Archie, and I can only like her for that. So I have been very tolerant and kind, and lent her a nightgown of my own and toiletries. But I will be glad when morning comes.

20th June

Uncle Cecil has promised Mimi he will do all he can to find out about Archie. He says they keep excellent records "over there" so if there is good news, it will reach us.

Honestly, how hard can it be to find someone? It's not as if Archie was there one minute and gone the next. That just isn't possible.

I have been given an appointment for my second interview at FANY headquarters – they call it "HQ" – but I have written to say that I cannot attend, due to circumstances beyond my control. That's a phrase Aunt Eloise suggested. I'm sure if they care enough to know exactly what circumstances, Aunt Leonora will fill them in.

23rd June

Terrible news. We have heard from one of Archie's fellow-cavalrymen that Firebrand is dead. He had two badly damaged legs, and was shot at close range, so the belief is that someone must have put the poor creature out of his misery. Was that Archie? Where *is* Archie? My eyes keep filling with tears and I cannot see to write any more.

24th June

I've had such a kind letter from the FANY office, sending their sympathy for my present difficulties, and saying they look forward to hearing further from me when circumstances permit. I can't imagine ever going there again.

28th June

There is still no news, but I will *not* give up hope. We have had just about all our relations to visit. Some are like us, still hoping for good news, but others are clearly trying to prepare us for the worst. They mean well, but I just know that Archie's out there, somewhere, alive.

Poor Mimi looks so sad. She has buried herself in her painting, and only emerges at mealtimes. Even then, I've had to send Elsie to fetch her more than once.

This evening, I reached across the dining table and laid a hand on hers. "How are you feeling, Mimi? Have you had a better day today?"

She took my hands between hers and said, "Don't worry about me, Daffy, darling. I'm perfectly well. Everyone's been so sweet."

"They have, haven't they?" I said.

"Mmm," she replied, as her soup was served. "Lalu and Polan have been particularly kind and consoling. I don't know what I would do without them."

Sometimes I wish I had a couple of fairies to make me feel better.

29th June

Mimi goes to the woods a lot. She's had many letters of consolation, and some people insist that Archie will return. There's even a letter from a clairvoyant – a friend of Mrs Hallibert's second cousin – who insists that she has seen the future. Archie will return, but he will be much changed. This sort of thing keeps Mimi going.

Me? I just wish I could go and look for him. Is *anybody* looking for him?

30th June

Today, Mimi asked me about the FANY.

"You should see about joining your little organization, Daffy darling," she said. "It would be good for you to do something useful. I know you roll your bandages, but—"

Goodness! That made me feel guilty.

"—but I'm sure it's not enough for you. You're an intelligent young woman."

Yes, I am, but I'm a horrible, careless, forgetful one. I haven't been bandage-rolling for ages. I will stop feeling sorry for myself and do something to help others.

4th July

I had forgotten how dreary bandage-rolling is. Thank heavens for a bit of light relief when we had a visit from one of the girls who went to work in the munitions factory. Her hand is heavily bandaged, but she's doing her best to keep cheerful.

"I was putting detonators in shells, like, to make them explode," she said. "I had to make a space in the shell, what was deep enough to hold the detonator, and I had to hit this metal spike thing with a big mallet. Only I missed the blinking spike and got two fingers and a thumb instead."

Oouch. But she was better off than her friend, who fell off a ladder and broke her whole arm!

Actually, it's odd to think that if I'd been there, I might have been able to help – I'm trained in first aid!

That evening I mentioned the FANY again to Mimi and Aunt Eloise.

Mimi smiled. "You join your FANY, Daffy darling. I know you feel the need to do something."

"But it would mean me going away," I said. "I expect I'd have to live in London for a while. Eaton Square, or maybe with Aunt Leonora."

"That's all right, darling," Mimi said. "I'll be fine. I won't be alone."

I smiled. "Of course, you'll have Aunt Eloise."

Mimi glanced up. "What? Oh yes, and Aunt Eloise, of course."

Those damn fairies.

7th July

I wrote to Aunt Leonora two days ago and have had a reply already. I'm to come to London and get myself sorted!

9th July

Aunt Leonora is a sweetie. She's very encouraging and thinks I should get going and join the FANY at once. "You're of good character," she said yesterday, at lunch. "You're marvellous at all sorts of physical things, and you don't give up easily." She hesitated. "Do you?"

I shook my head rapidly. I don't give up easily, really – it's just that I don't always get started.

"Then you'll be perfect. We'll go back to Earl's Court Road this very afternoon."

"I don't have an appointment," I said.

"Yes you have. I made one for you. Just in case."

And so we did. Two of the officer women were there before and remembered me.

"We knew you'd be back," said one.

"Yes," said the other. "You can always tell a girl with backbone."

My driving report was in and they said that apart from a tendency to recklessness, I am basically cool, calm, and competent behind the wheel, and that is where they see my future. As a driver!

My first-aid report said I take tuition well, but must try not to let my emotional nature get the better of my practical side. That's probably because I kept going, "Oh, ugh, I couldn't do that," and making being-sick noises.

"We'll call that a pass," said the chief interviewer, with a twinkle in her eye. "There'll be plenty of nurses where you're going, so let's hope your first-aid, um, skills won't be needed!"

So, the upshot is that I'm in. I've paid my dues and I'm a member of FANY! Tomorrow we go to Gamage's to buy my uniform, and then Bobby's going to take me to a photographer friend of hers, to have my photograph taken in my uniform.

I wonder where they'll send me. Obviously near a hospital.

10th July

I loved Gamage's. We had an appointment with a fitter, and until then we wandered round looking at all the different things you can buy. I think if I lived in London my allowance would be gone in a week!

I adore my uniform. The skirt is quite short, just ten inches from the ground is the rule, and there's a lovely hat. It's soft, and divided into four quarters that are gathered together on to a band with a badge on it! The badge of the

FANY is a Maltese cross in a circle, and is very bold and easily recognized. I shall feel like somebody who matters when I wear my uniform (which I did as soon as we got back to Aunt Leonora's). I don't have the badges and things yet, but Aunt Leonora's going to hang on to the uniform and get it all sorted ready for next week when I report for duty.

Actually, I wasn't sorry to take the tunic off. It's frightfully itchy. I shall have to speak to Elsie about some nice silky underwear.

13th July

I have resigned from the bandage-rollers, written notes to anyone I think might like to know that I've gone, and am moving to Aunt Leonora's tomorrow. I am sad to say goodbye to Mimi and Aunt Eloise, and very sad to say goodbye to Billie and Honeycomb and even Gulliver. Aunt Eloise has promised to be especially kind to Billie, and will let him sleep at her door, as he does at mine.

Mimi has come over all anxious again, because I am to be attached to the FANY office for the time being, on driving duties!

"Do be careful driving in London, Daffy darling," she said.

"It's probably very dangerous. Watch out for the horses and the omnibuses."

On driving duties! How exciting!

A note was delivered this evening by a footman from Great Oaks. At first I thought it was from Elizabeth Baguley, but then realized that was most unlikely. She won't miss me. No, it was from Reggie, saying he's so sorry I'm leaving, and would love to see me in London. Isn't that nice? But I shall be far too busy.

14th July

I left this morning in absolute floods of tears, swearing to take great care of myself, and behaving not at all like a member of a wartime organization. Snap out of it, Daffy!

19th July

Driving duties are deadly dull. The only excitement is when an aeroplane goes over and everyone runs for cover. This has a bad effect on my nerves.

I've had to attend a lot of lectures, and I do have trouble staying awake in some of them. One or two of the lecturers were superb, though, and made everything sound thrilling, even something as odd as arranging for Tommies, as they call our soldiers, to bath in the back of a special vehicle. Forty men an hour can have a bath, miles from any hotel or anything. It's amazing – I saw pictures of it. It has collapsible baths in the back, and the water is heated by the engine, in a sort of tank! Amazing! I should get an engine like that at home – it takes Elsie hours to fetch and heat enough water just for me!

Oh dear, thinking of Elsie makes me sad. I shall go downstairs and play cards with Bobby when she comes home. I hope I don't get a lecture from *her*! She's deadly earnest about rights and votes and things. I agree with everything she says, but I'm glad there are other people fighting that particular battle.

31st July

I am so excited, and a little afraid. Three days ago, I was called into the FANY office and told that I am to be sent to France!

"You're an excellent driver," they said. "We'd better send you out there as soon as possible. Get ready for the off, Rowntree."

Gosh, that was a little unexpected. I'm to report to the FANY convoy in Calais, and eventually I'm to become an ambulance driver.

I'm not used to things happening so quickly. How will I ever be ready in time? Will they like me? Will I fit in?

I immediately went home to sort everything out and to break the news to Mimi and Aunt Eloise. I'm not giving them much detail. I know soldiers are supposed to be careful of what they say because of spies. Well, I'm in the armed forces now (except I'm not armed), so perhaps I should keep my movements secret. I decided to tell Mimi the truth, that I'm going to Calais, and that Calais is miles from the front line where the fighting is. My guess was that she wouldn't ask exactly how far, and I was right.

My lovely mother's reaction was to hug me and say, "Daffy darling, life is very short. We mortals should make the most of our brief time, Lalu says. You must do what makes you happy."

I told her that I'm not doing this to make me happy, I'm doing it out of patriotic duty!

"While you're in France, Daffy," she said, "you will look for Archie, won't you?"

"Oh, Mimi," I said, "his own regiment can't find him. How will I? I shall be nowhere near the front line, where he was last seen. That's where they found Firebrand, remember?"

"No, darling, I don't remember," she said, picking up some pine cones she'd brought in from the garden to paint.

She doesn't want to remember, poor thing.

As I left, Aunt Eloise hugged me and pressed some cash into my hand. "You look very smart in your uniform, Daffy," she said. "Now off you go. Stay safe."

I dripped all over Billie, who looked so sad. There is nothing quite so pathetic as an unhappy Airedale.

Then Mimi kissed me goodbye. Her last words were, "Find my Archie."

I wish I could. Is it possible?

2nd August

I've had the most ghastly day. I stayed overnight with Aunt Leonora and got to Folkestone with no problem except for a horrendous thunderstorm. I was with two other FANYs, Corbett and Sutton, who'd been home on leave and were returning to Calais. They were very jolly, which was nice at first, but I fail to see how anyone could stay *that* perky in such conditions. I stood on the windswept quay, my tunic soaked, and my skirt flapping damply around my calves. Our sailing was delayed because some mines had come loose in the water, and it was too dangerous. If we'd hit them, they'd have blown up – and us with them.

Eventually we were allowed to board, and soon we were able to stand at the rail and wave goodbye to anyone who'd wave back. I was so glad to be on the boat.

But not for long. Oh, I'd forgotten how dreadfully seasick I can be. I have never felt so ill in my life, not even when Archie and I ate some red berries we found in the shrubbery. Corbett thought it was hilarious, though Sutton was a little more sympathetic.

"Come on, Rowntree," said Corbett. "You can't start off like a wet lettuce. Take deep breaths."

As every breath I took was damp and tasted of oil, I ignored her and instead took Sutton's advice. I found a bench, lay down and closed my eyes. The only time I opened them was to raise my head to check that the destroyers accompanying us were still in sight. Although being targeted by a German submarine might put an end to my misery, it was something I didn't want to think about too much.

But it didn't last. I lived through that hideous journey and am now in France. It's just as wet here. Corbett, Sutton and I finally arrived in camp late this afternoon, and we don't start duties until tomorrow. Just as well. How I'm ever going to make myself comfortable in this place, I cannot imagine. When I looked round our hut – for that's all it is – I said, "Gosh, this is a bit grim!"

One of the girls, Meldrew, stuck her head out of her cubicle and said, "You've got a nerve! It wasn't long ago we were living in tents among the sand dunes."

"Too right," said another, called Jolliphant. "The tents used to belong to the Army in India, so they weren't suited to the perishing winds we get up here."

"And the tent pegs wouldn't hold in the sand," said Meldrew. "Many's the night I woke to find my tent blown halfway out to sea. In the end, I moved into an old bathing machine. Dingy and damp and smelly, but at least it was still there when I came to in the mornings."

Personally I think the hut is dingy and smelly, but it certainly isn't damp. There's an oil stove absolutely shoving out heat – the air's thick with it, and I suppose I should be grateful. At least I was able to dry out my tunic and skirt.

Jolliphant showed me my cubicle. It has a bed, like a cot, and a sleeping bag – or "flea-bag" as Meldrew calls it. I have some shelves, and little else. There's a bathroom at the end of the hut, but it's so *basic*.

What have I done?

3rd August

When everyone was asleep last night, I had a little cry.

I felt better this morning. At least, I do now. We were roused at some unearthly hour – we washed and dressed at the speed of light (oh, Elsie, I will never snap at you again), and went straight outside for roll call. This was before breakfast!

Meldrew explained roll call. It's just to make sure everybody's up and ready for work. I understand that, but surely it would be as quick – and a lot more pleasant – if we simply checked each other. But I'm not in a position to suggest changes yet.

The other thing she told me was to salute the FANY officer in charge – everyone calls her Boss – first thing in the morning, but I needn't bother again during the day.

"We're a bit different from other military outfits," Meldrew explained. "We're a lot more informal, but," she added, seeing my expression, "you needn't think that means we're slackers. We get things done."

"I'm sure," I said politely.

"Someone once said that FANY meant First ANYwhere," Meldrew continued. "Let's see if we can be first to brekker." And off she raced. She's fun!

We had breakfast – or "brekker" as I must learn to call it – in a hut called the mess. It's quite tidy really, but that's what it's called. We had porridge, which I love (though the tin bowl was not too pleasant), and I was halfway through mine when someone outside bellowed, "Barges! Barges!"

Honestly, you'd have thought the place was on fire. In seconds, everyone was on their feet, heading for the door.

"What is it? What's happening?" I cried.

Meldrew shoved me out of the way. "Barges. You stay here."

In no time, the only people left in the hut were me, the cook and an orderly – her assistant – who are both FANY members, too. All I could hear was a steady booming in the distance.

The cook, who has bobbed hair and seems frightfully modern, explained what "barges" means. "Wounded Tommies from the front have to be brought to safety for treatment. Most of them come on special trains, but the worst ones travel on barges on the canal. It makes the journey less bumpy for the poor souls."

"So "Barges!" means some barges have arrived?" I said.

"Right." The cook handed me a cotton cloth. "The girls have to drive helter-skelter down to the quay, collect the patients, and take them to one of the Calais hospitals or to a ship." She stopped what she was doing and said, "Dishes?"

I thought this was another technical term. "What's "dishes"?" I asked, keen to learn.

Merriwether, the orderly, burst out laughing. "It's those upside-down wet things that everyone's just eaten their porridge out of. Dry them!"

I've never done dishes before. It's quite relaxing.

Afterwards, we sat and had a cup of tea (well, a mug, actually – there are no cups here) and I told the others about Archie. They were so sympathetic.

"My mother wants me to look for him," I said.

They stared. "Rowntree," said the cook, who's been a

FANY since before the war, "I don't want to dash your hopes, but if he's not been found by now, my dear, he probably isn't going to be. And anyway, you're going to be far too busy here to go searching for your brother."

"But I could, you know, sort of keep my eyes open, couldn't I? He might be in a hospital, suffering from loss of memory or something. I could ask if there are any young men with no names."

Merriwether poured milk into my empty cup. I hate that. I like to add the milk to the tea.

"He could be a prisoner of the Germans, I suppose," she said. "You needn't give up hope, Rowntree."

I was grateful to her for saying that, but I could see the cook thinks I'm off my chump.

Just then another FANY burst in through the door. She had bobbed hair, too. "Rowntree! Welcome to our convoy," she said. "There's a car outside that could do with a lick. Just the wheels till we've time to take it into town. Jump to it."

She spoke so briskly and disappeared so quickly I didn't have time to ask what she meant. I looked helplessly at Merriwether.

She laughed. "Come on, I'll show you."

Before I knew what was happening, I found myself with a bucket of water, cloth and brush and a car. The wheels were absolutely caked with mud. I wonder anyone had been able to drive it.

"Slosh some water on them," said Merriwether. "The girls

95

usually take the cars into town to be washed properly, so you needn't fuss too much. Here, I'll give you a hand."

I examined the car. The front seat was just a board with a couple of worn cushions on it. There was no windscreen, and in the back, the seats had been taken out and the space divided into four sections – two up and two down. It had a canvas roof.

"What is it?" I asked.

Merriwether stared at me. "It's an ambulance, you mutt! What did you think it was? It holds four stretchers in the back for four *blessés*."

"*Blessés*?"

"It's French. It means casualties. It's what we call the patients."

"I see." I walked round the front. "Why is there no windscreen? The driver might get a fly in her eye."

I soon learned that there was no windscreen for very good reasons. They might reflect light at night, and the enemy might see it and shoot. Also, it could get hit by a stone, never mind a bullet, and shatter, which could injure the driver.

When I'd finished, Merriwether suggested I go to our hut and clean the bathroom. I decided to write in my diary first. Now that I'm sitting here in France, all on my own, I miss everyone so much. I keep thinking of Mimi, pining for Archie.

I won't go searching for him. I believe the cook's right. There can be little hope. But then Merriwether told me not to give up hope. Well, I won't. I won't go searching, but I'll never stop looking.

Later

I fell asleep! And I hadn't even started the bathroom, which was absolutely filthy. I didn't know where to begin. There was a cloth lying on the floor beside the basin, so I used that. Lots of water, and a bit of soap for the really mucky bits, and it was done.

In the corner of the hut I found a broom. I'd seen the maids use one often enough, and I even used to help Hawkins sweep the yard when I was small, so I knew what to do. Picking up all the dirt and fluff wasn't easy. I shoved it on to a magazine and tipped it in a bin. Then I used the cloth to wash over the floor. I could see it would all take a while to dry, so I left the door and windows open.

Just as I was finishing, there was the roar of motors. I looked out and saw several ambulances pulling up. When the girls got out, I was shocked at the state of them. They were pale, and their hair stuck out all over the place, their belts were undone and they looked as if they could hardly walk for tiredness. They'd only been gone a few hours.

Most headed for their huts. Meldrew came in and flung herself on her bed. I stood in the doorway, clutching the broom.

"Hello, Cinders," she said wearily. "Been busy?"

Others were coming in now and collapsing on their beds. I thought I might have another little lie-down myself, but decided I didn't deserve it, so I went back to the cookhouse.

I was set to work peeling potatoes. It's not an easy job at all, and your hands get very cold and covered with dirty water. But I did feel as if I was helping to cook the dinner.

We hadn't spoken for a while, when Merriwether suddenly said, "What's that hideous noise?"

I looked up from my "spuds" as they're called here. "It's the fighting at the front," I said. "I thought it was thunder when I arrived."

She laughed. "I didn't mean that." Cocking her head to one side, she listened. "It's stopped now."

I went back to my spud-peeling.

After a moment or two, Merriwether said, "There it is again – that noise. What on earth is it?"

I didn't reply, because I was trying to hold back a giggle. The noise was me, humming!

The rest of the day passed in a series of small jobs, some of which I did well, and some of which I couldn't begin to understand. At one point, I was given something called "Little Mary Custard Powder". I hadn't a clue what to do with it, until Merriwether kindly showed me. As milk isn't too plentiful at the moment I had to use half milk and half water. It looked quite nice when I'd finished, but the cook just glanced at it and handed me a whisk to get the lumps out. I didn't realize cooking was so complicated. I suppose they're the sort of tasks our servants do all the time, but it's all right for them – they've been trained.

7th August

The drivers are divided into two sections, and as I'm going to be a driver I'm in one of them. Our section leader is Corbett, and she's a sergeant. She's very friendly, though, and only gets bossy when someone's slacking. And that's not very often, I can tell you. These FANYs are a great group of girls. Bags of energy!

It's quite a tiring life, though.

Another new girl, from the other section, and I had a little talk from her section leader, explaining the system for the wounded men. They're treated first at a dressing station, then get sent to a casualty clearing station. From there they go either to the train or the canal quay to be transported down to us. That's when we pick them up and deliver them to hospitals or the ships for home. Some of them don't survive the journey, the section leader explained, so it's obvious what sort of state they're in, and we must be kind, compassionate and as gentle as possible. But we have to be firm, too.

16th August

My cubicle is a little nicer now. Mimi has sent me three postcards from home, which she has decorated herself – with fairies, of course.

"Aah! Aren't they sweet!" Meldrew said.

Jolliphant and some of the others crowded in to see what she was talking about. They loved them, too. I think I'll ask Mimi to send a little picture to Meldrew for her birthday, which is very soon.

I've spent nearly all my time on orderly duties, which involves mostly housework-type things. One thing I've learned is to use the right tool for the job. For instance, there's a special sharp knife thingy for doing potatoes – you don't use an ordinary dinner knife. And there are special cloths that you use for cleaning. I will never, ever forget the roar from Jolliphant!

"Has some *clown* been using my face cloth to wash their motor car?"

I kept quiet. She shouldn't have left it on the bathroom floor.

I might be driving soon, the Boss said. One of the girls has gone back to Blighty (that's what they call England). She has compassionate leave, because the man she was engaged to has been killed. Being one pair of hands short makes a difference, and we're going to get very busy now, Corbett says.

The last couple of weeks have been quieter than usual, I'm told, because there hasn't been nearly as much fighting going on at the front. I can't imagine what it must be like when it's really busy. I'm absolutely worn out all the time. I've never worked so hard in my life. I swear I will be more thoughtful towards our servants when I go home.

Anyway, the reason it's been quieter is that the weather has been so appalling. Rain, rain and more rain. Apparently, the battlefield at the front is just a sea of mud, and it's dotted with huge shell-holes which are like craters filled with water.

One of the girls, Westerling, said gloomily, "When that lot dries out they're going to find a fair number of bodies in the craters."

I thought of Archie. I had to run to the bathroom, where I was violently sick.

18th August

Today I feel so tired. My eyes burn and my head throbs. I'm to stay in the hut for a couple of hours this morning, to rest, and then I'm to go and help in the cookhouse.

The reason for my feelings of exhaustion? Partly it's because yesterday I actually went to the war. Well, not to it, exactly, but up near the front line. I had my first drive in one of the ambulances, to see what I'm made of, as they put it. I went with Jolliphant to take comforts up to the troops. The FANY don't just do ambulance duties, they take supplies, drive nurses to and from the boat so they can go home on leave – all sorts of things. Even collecting laundry for the hospitals! We can use army cars for driving the army nurses – much more comfortable! One thing surprised me – sometimes we're expected to take wounded German prisoners to a hospital.

"The FANY are known for doing anything they have to do," said Meldrew proudly.

"Including peeling spuds!" I laughed.

Anyway, there I was, up front in the ambulance, on its very hard seat, with Jolliphant at my side. I'd started the vehicle on the seventeenth swing of the starting handle, which wasn't bad!

Outside the town, we approached a level crossing.

"Always watch it here," Jolliphant warned. "They're using local women as crossing-keepers, and they're useless. This one's called Sleepy Suzanne, because she always comes out yawning and stretching as if she's just got out of bed. Even if she signals you to go across, check both ways!"

The crossing-keeper ambled out of her cottage, just as Jolliphant had said.

"Once," Jolliphant said, breaking off to shout a quick, "*Merci, madame,*" to the crossing-keeper, "Sutton couldn't rouse Sleepy Suzanne, so she got out of the ambulance and went on to the track to throw a stone up at the window. A train came along, and poor Sutton had to scramble over the barrier to safety!"

I'd picked up speed and we were bowling merrily along. "It won't all be like this," said Jolliphant. "We're going fairly close to the front. It's not pretty, I warn you."

So far it had been very pretty. We'd had a nice view of the sea to start with, then passed through a dear little village with a very old church. But as we rumbled forward, things began to change. Houses stood empty, with gardens overgrown. Those that weren't shuttered had broken windows.

"You're going to see far worse than that," said Jolliphant, hearing me tutting at such a shambles. "You're not half a good driver, though, Rowntree."

"Thanks," I said. It was the first compliment I'd had since I arrived.

She was absolutely right. The further we travelled, the worse the landscape became. We stopped by a crumbled wall for a call of nature. There was a broken kitchen table lying nearby.

"I'll leave the engine running, so I don't have to start it again," I said. My arm still ached.

"OK," said Jolliphant. "I'll stay here till you've finished."

"That's awfully decent of you," I said, appreciating the privacy.

She snorted. "It's not for your sake, it's so our precious ambulance doesn't get pinched by the Germans."

"*What*?"

"Tell you in a sec," she said. "Get a move on. My turn."

I was suddenly aware that the rumbling, booming noise that was always in the background was much louder here. "Is that gunfire?" I called.

"Probably round Ypres," she said.

"Is that where the fighting is?" I asked, returning to the ambulance.

"Lord, Rowntree, where do you bury your head? It must be awfully quiet there, wherever it is. Don't you have *any* idea what's going on? Of course that's where the fighting is. It's the third battle we've fought there. It's been going on for weeks!" She strode behind the wall. "I don't know. What an innocent."

I don't object to her calling me an innocent. If she'd called me ignorant she'd have been spot on. I feel quite ashamed. I tried to excuse myself by saying, "Everybody said the fighting had all but stopped since I arrived, so I haven't really been aware of it."

"You will be now."

Soon we were back on the road, if you could call it a road. It was a disgrace – full of potholes, and with a dangerous ditch each side. Every time we passed another vehicle – which wasn't often, thank goodness – I was scared my right wheels would slide over the edge.

"What's this about Germans?" I asked eventually. "They're all at the front line, surely?"

"That's what you hope. But some are taken prisoner and manage to escape. Some crash their planes and go on the run. You never can tell. Better safe than sorry, that's my watchword."

Mine too, now. I'd hate to meet a German.

The booming of the guns was much louder now, and I'd been noticing the landscape changing. We passed many houses and cottages that were all but ruined. There couldn't have been anybody living in them. Jolliphant told me they'd probably been hit by shells or stray bombs.

My stomach lurched when she said that. If shells and bombs reached this far, then we could be in danger. And it was clear they could. There was hardly a tree standing. Well, there were lots of blackened tree trunks, but few had any branches or leaves on them. "Shell damage?" I said.

"Shells," agreed Jolliphant. "And fire."

The sky was darkening. I looked round at the damaged houses and ruined farm buildings. There was nothing growing in the fields – they were just grass and weeds and mud, endless mud. I thought back to the factory girl who'd hammered her hand. This was the sort of damage her shells caused. What would they do if they hit a soldier?

105

A picture of Archie and Firebrand flashed into my mind. I thrust it away. It was too much to bear, and I had to concentrate on just staying on the road.

Nearer and nearer the front we went, passing more and more vehicles and sometimes local people on foot, who waved. They didn't smile, though. They looked too tired for that. Occasionally the gunfire almost stopped for a moment, but then started again, pounding away at my brain. I tried to imagine each bang was a bullet or a shell, but it became too much to contemplate.

Rain began to fall. Thin spiteful drops. I wished we had a proper windscreen.

Almost there.

"Look!" Jolliphant cried suddenly.

I stamped on the brake. "What?" My heart pounded.

"Men," she said. "Break open a couple of boxes, quickly. We'll give them some comforts. They look like they need them, poor souls."

I jumped out of my seat and ran round the back. "But why? These are for the soldiers at the front."

"Rowntree, these men *are* soldiers," Jolliphant explained, not too patiently, as she grabbed a couple of boxes.

As the line of men drew level with us, I could see the exhaustion in their faces. They were filthy, and their uniforms stiffly caked with mud. Jolliphant explained they'd been in the trenches for days and were being marched off to the small town nearby for some rest and good food.

"Be prepared for a bit of a pong," she said. "They probably haven't washed for weeks."

She chatted cheerfully to the men as she handed out cigarettes and tobacco. They were so pleased to have them, though I can't think why. Smoking has always seemed a revolting pastime to me.

I gave out scarves. I smiled and chatted, too, though the smell of the men was getting to me. One middle-aged man took a scarf, but said, "Got any socks instead, Miss? I couldn't half do with some dry socks. It's like a swamp up there in the trenches. Stinks like one, too, begging yer pardon, Miss."

Jolliphant heard. "There are some in the back, Rowntree," she called.

I went to look and the man followed me. Suddenly there was an eerie whistling sound, followed by a mighty explosion. I stood rooted, frozen to the spot. "Wh-what was that?"

"Stray shell, Miss," he said. "Not too close. Don't you worry none. It can't do you no harm now."

I took a deep breath and tried to look as relaxed as he was. But my hands shook as I broke open a package.

"My feet've been sloshing about in watery mud for days now," said the man. "Reckon they're going rotten, I do, Miss."

I pulled out some dark green socks. There was a little message tied to them, which he examined eagerly. I remembered the knitting group adding little messages to their completed items. How lovely to know that they were so appreciated.

"Gawd bless you, Miss," he said. "Hey! You lot! There's socks round the back here!"

In seconds I was thrusting socks into eager hands. They were so grateful it made me wish I'd tried a bit harder with my knitting.

We drove on.

"Where does all the mud come from?" I asked. "We have rain at home but it never gets like this."

"I wondered that when I first came," said Jolliphant. "It's because the area's low-lying and very wet, so to keep the marshy land suitable for farming, the locals put in drainage systems. The shells smash the pipes, so the land doesn't drain. Thus you get mud. And believe me, the nearer you go to the front, the worse it gets. Especially after all the rainstorms we've had. I don't know, this is supposed to be summer!"

Occasionally planes buzzed overhead. They always took me by surprise – I couldn't hear them over the noise of my engine.

"Look at all those huge puddles," I said, as I slowed to manoeuvre round a particularly large one that spread over half the road.

"They're not puddles," said Jolliphant, "so don't you dare drive into one. They're shell holes, and they're deep. You'll be up to your neck in muddy water before you know it. And it stinks."

"Gosh, that's dangerous!"

108

"You think this is dangerous?" said Jolliphant. "Between our front trenches and the German front trenches, there's no-man's-land. It's full of shell holes, and when the men scramble out of their trenches to attack the Germans, some of them fall into the holes, which are usually full of water."

I remembered what Westerling said about finding corpses in the shell holes when they dried out.

"But if they fall in, they can climb out?" I asked.

She looked at me for a moment. "Rowntree, the reason they fall in is usually because they're wounded. Sometimes they can't get out, and that's it – they're goners. Others fall into the mud when they're shot. And the worst thing is," she continued, "that when the next lot of men come charging behind them, they can't see where they're going for smoke and mud and rain, and trample on the fallen ones, whether they're dead or alive."

I was silent. I couldn't cope with this.

Jolliphant punched my arm. "Come on, Rowntree, let her rip!"

I put my foot down. Almost immediately, she cried, "Slow down!"

Something lay ahead, half on the road and half off. Nearby was a group of cavalrymen, most still mounted. One of them was kneeling beside the object. As we drew closer, I saw that it was a horse, dead. One of its hind legs had been blown away. The soldier looked up at us, tears glittering in his eyes.

109

I went to stop, but Jolliphant said, "Keep going. The horse must have been caught by a shell. There's nothing we can do."

I heard what she said, but my heart was somersaulting. These men were cavalry. They might know Archie! I braked, and the ambulance slithered to a stop on the muddy road surface. I leapt out.

"Archie Rowntree! Archibald! My brother! Do you know him?" I shouted to the cavalrymen. "Have you seen him?"

Slowly, they shook their heads.

"Sorry, Miss," said one. "I've never heard of him."

I burst into tears. "But he can't have just disappeared. He can't!" Visions of shell holes, bodies trodden into mud, and dead horses whirled through my head. I felt faint.

Jolliphant's arm went round me as she guided me back to the ambulance. "Sit here. I'll drive," she said.

I sat beside her and sobbed. I thought I'd cried enough for Archie and Papa, but I hadn't. That wasn't real crying. This was. It came from somewhere deep inside me. And it hurt so much.

The rest of the trip passed, but I remember only a little. Grateful men. Ruined villages. French people trudging along the road, heads bowed. And over it all, the constant boom of the guns. Boom-boom-boom.

I curled up in my flea-bag when we got back to camp. Meldrew brought me some cocoa and said things would look better in the morning. They do, a little.

The Boss came and talked to me, and although I didn't want to, I found myself telling her all about Archie, and how Mimi's convinced he's alive.

"And you, Rowntree?" she said. "What do you think?"

I swallowed hard. "I think he must be dead. But I'll never stop looking."

21st August

I'm an absolute disaster in the kitchen. Never again will I complain to Mrs Rose that the toast is cold, and never again will I look at a table laden with food and tell the maid that what I'd really like is some scrambled eggs. We're only cooking for about twenty at a time. Imagine poor Mrs Rose cooking for all our family, and cooking different things for the servants – three times a day! Not to mention all the bottling of fruit, and the baking of cakes and biscuits and so on. And, oh dear, my late-evening requests for hot milk, when the poor woman's probably ready for bed. Maybe even *in* bed, exhausted.

Like me. I get so tired these days that I just fall into bed. Well, on it. It's not very soft, but my flea-bag is comforting, and I'm getting used to it. The same as I'm getting used to the roll calls, and the rushing about, and all the on-the-spot lessons, like how to do things with spark plugs (haven't quite got to grips with that yet) and all about grease guns and exhausts and wrenches. I've learned to change a wheel, and have been challenged to do it in ten minutes. Some hopes.

I even know how to get stains off clothes with petrol! That's something to tell Elsie when I get home, although it might not be so good there, as the smell is awful.

We do have a couple of mechanics to call on, but we're expected to look after the cars (that's what ambulances are called) ourselves. We have to put oil and water in, and do all sorts of things with the engine that I haven't mastered yet.

But I will.

23rd August

Meldrew bobbed Jolliphant's hair this evening. I must say, it looks jolly smart, even though it's a bit ragged at the ends. Meldrew said it will grow into itself, whatever that means.

As soon as it was dark, we drove down to the sea for a swim. It was glorious! Afterwards, we dried ourselves and dressed behind the ambulance. Jolliphant made a big show of towelling her hair dry, saying what a wonderful relief it was to have it so light and short. When she'd finished, she looked like an upended floor mop.

25th August

Today was my first day of driving wounded men. Just one barge was coming in, and four ambulances went down. I drove one of them. I was pretty nervous. I just wanted to do it right, especially after my outburst when Jolliphant and I took supplies up near the front lines.

It's been a bright, breezy day, not too hot, so everyone set off in high spirits for the canal quay. I was second, and had no trouble keeping up with Meldrew, in the lead. Maybe it's the way the wind was blowing, or maybe my engine was quieter than usual, but as I drove I could still hear the endless booming of the guns, far away.

When we got to the quayside, we manoeuvred into position, backing towards the canal, and waited. Before too long, the barge appeared, gliding quietly through the water.

While they were bringing the *blessés* up on their stretchers, I peeped inside. It was just like a hospital ward. I think the men must have been as comfortable as possible on their journey down, although several didn't appear to be conscious.

The attendants were so kind and gentle. They carefully slid the stretchers into the backs of our ambulances, and soon both Meldrew and I were ready for the off.

There's a slope up from the canal. I tried desperately hard to start away smoothly, and I don't think it was too bad. The roads are dreadful here, and it's hard to steer round potholes and keep the ride smooth at the same time. Occasionally, when I was unable to avoid a bump, one of the men would groan, which made me feel terrible. These poor men had come by barge especially so they wouldn't have to suffer on a jolting train ride. Now I was putting them through unnecessary pain.

I was shaking by the time I reached the hospital, and was so relieved to have the staff there take over. As my *blessés* were lifted out, two of them managed to lift a heavy hand and say, "Thanks, Miss."

"Goodbye and God bless," I said. Tears pricked my eyes. The men had bloodstained bandages and moaned quietly as they were moved. And all they had to look forward to, once they'd recovered, was being sent back to the trenches to face the guns again.

In spite of that, and in spite of their dreadful injuries, I couldn't help wishing that one of them was my brother.

It was only as I climbed back into the driving seat that I realized how tense I'd been on the journey. My knees and my back felt rigid and ached so.

"Let's go, Rowntree!" shouted Meldrew, and off we went. It was a much better, and much faster drive back – three times faster, in fact, and I actually found myself enjoying handling the car. We used a different road on the way back, so there was no chance we'd crash into another ambulance making its slow and steady way with its precious cargo of *blessés*.

Two more trips and I was done. All that was left to do was take some stretcher-bearers back to their quarters.

When we arrived at camp, Sutton came over to me and said, "First time for you, Rowntree, wasn't it? Well done, old thing!"

All my life, outsiders have sometimes disapproved of me and my behaviour. Here was someone telling me I'd done well. I don't think I've ever felt such pride. Meldrew says I'm a "bird", which I gather is the opposite of "blighter", so that's all right!

I do like it here. It's hard, but I feel it's right for me. I think I fit.

I reached the hut to find some mail waiting for me. Another postcard from Mimi, which was pounced on by some of the girls before I'd even read it, with cries of, "Oh, aren't they *sweet*!" Needless to say, Lalu and some of her little friends featured prominently in the decoration. Mimi asked if I had been looking for Archie.

Yes, Mimi, but only every time I step outside the camp. Only every time I pass some men on the road. And now that

I am to be on permanent ambulance duty, only every time a stretcher is put into my car.

There was a letter from Bobby, telling me she was jolly proud of me, and that it's perfectly splendid that I'm helping our boys. And there was a sad little note from Violet. She says her heart is quite broken, and she has started a second knitting group in the next village.

Clever Violet. As Archie once said, isn't she amazing? Oh, stop being so nasty, Daffy.

I kept a little package to myself, and didn't open it in front of the others. I could feel what was inside it.

It was only when I stopped to think about today that I realized I hadn't much noticed the booming of the guns. I was getting used to it. I told Jolliphant, and she said the only time she ever noticed the guns was when they stopped.

30th August

It was Meldrew's birthday today. The rest of us got up early and, since we don't have any bunting, strung our most colourful undies across the room. When she woke, she burst out laughing and said we were all absolute buffoons.

After roll call and brekker, she opened her presents.

Several people had made things for her. Jolliphant had stolen Meldrew's plain white petticoat weeks before, and had spent hours and hours in secret, embroidering it with pansies. Corbett gave her *Something Fresh* by P G Wodehouse, who is screamingly funny. We all want to borrow that! Then there was a little book of poetry from Westerling, and a third book, which is of plain cream paper for her to write in. That was from Sutton, who's always writing in such a book herself. She says she will be a great novelist one day.

I would have liked that notebook. My diary is rather battered, and has two small oil-stains on the silk cover.

Soon it was my turn to give her a present. I took out the contents of the little package Mimi had sent, crossed my fingers and said I hoped she'd like it. Meldrew pulled at the tissue paper it was wrapped in, then gave a little scream.

"Rowntree! You darling! It's one of your mother's paintings! What's it called? It's written here..." She squinted at the pencilled writing at the bottom, near the frame. "'Lalu and her baby!' Oh how perfectly adorable!"

She jumped up and hugged me. "Thanks, old bird! Cripes, a genuine Rowntree painting!"

These girls are so nice. Why have I never found friends like them before?

It was only after the lights were put out that I realized Lalu had had a baby. Whatever next?

29th September

I haven't had a free moment to myself for ages. At least, I haven't had a free moment in which I was able to stay awake! The *blessés* have been pouring down from the front. It must be utter carnage up there. The good news is that the British, with the help of other nations, have made progress against the Germans. The bad news is that it's at such a terrible cost. We only see the live casualties. How many dead must there be?

I'm so thankful for a breather. I sometimes wonder how much longer I can go on. Every day has started at some unearthly hour, with trains or barges to meet. Sometimes we've been woken in the middle of the night because word's come that a train's on its way. Often we're at the railway sidings long before the train arrives, and have to wait for hours. Then there are anything up to 400 wounded men to transport. The nights are really cold now, and there always seems to be a sharp wind coming off the sea. Driving at night, apart from being cold, strains my eyes. As we can't use headlights, we have to drive with our noses practically on the bonnet in order to see where we're going, and to avoid the worst of the holes in the roads. All this might be against a background of heart-rending groans, or some poor lad screaming for his mother. I yearn to race to the hospital or ship, to get them there quicker, but I know it's better to go slowly, to take them gently.

Even when we stagger into the mess hut for a bite to eat, there's hardly time for a cup of cocoa before someone's sent off on a special job, delivering an officer here, fetching someone from there, collecting supplies from the boats and delivering them to the hospitals. Or, worst of all, "doing corpses". That means transporting dead bodies to the mortuary. I try not to think of them as people. That seems hard, I know, but if I do start imagining their lives and families, it almost destroys me. So I don't.

Never mind. I'm going home on leave soon.

14th October

My leave was almost as exhausting as life in camp.

Mimi says she's fine. I actually think she is better, because her latest lot of paintings are beginning to show some of the old boldness. There's a fairy in every one, but that's all right, because the Americans are still buying them. So Uncle Cecil told me when I visited him and Aunt Leonora briefly. Bobby whirled in and whirled out, just pausing to say, "I think you're perfectly splendid, Daffers. Get your hair cut." Hers is even shorter now – almost as short as a man's. It does look awfully dashing, though.

Aunt Leonora's heard good things about me! I'm so proud. She said I seem to have knuckled down and adapted beautifully, and I'm not afraid to tackle anything. I didn't tell her that my mechanical maintenance leaves a lot to be desired, and I couldn't cope without Meldrew and Merriwether helping and guiding me. Well, without them doing a lot of it, actually.

The FANY don't require me to do lectures yet, but I did have to go fundraising. I went with a couple of girls as they addressed small audiences. I hope I never have to do that – even with only twenty or thirty people, it would scare me to death. I'd rather take Honeycomb over our yew hedge with no stirrups than speak in public.

Dear Honeycomb! She was so pleased to see me. Billie, I was annoyed to notice, adores Aunt Eloise, but he did give me a glorious welcome. Gulliver grabbed the chunk of crusty bread I took him, then, as I chatted to Hawkins, chewed my skirt. So everything's normal.

Aunt Eloise said Mimi's talk is often about other things now, not just fairies. I was wrong about Lalu having a baby. She has three. I've seen a painting of them, and they are unbelievably dainty and pretty – all girls!

I can't believe I wrote that last sentence! Whatever is the matter with me? Jolly good thing I'm back in camp. That steady booming of the guns keeps reminding me why I'm here.

15th October

A huge hank of my hair came unpinned today while I was cleaning my engine and, when I brought my head up, it was all oily.

When Jolliphant saw it, she said, "Hmm, there's only one sensible course of action, Rowntree, old thing."

"What's that?"

"Meldrewww!" she bawled. "Fetch the scissors!"

"No!" I squealed, but everyone joined in chanting, "Bob! Bob! Bob!" and I suppose I remembered what Bobby said and got swept away with it all. Anyway, here I sit in my cubicle, half afraid to look in the mirror, but absolutely delighted with the result!

16th October

Oh dear. I had a little note from Reggie today. It was mainly news of the Baguleys and their social life, but it ended with a rather peeved comment about how he didn't see me when I was on leave. I wouldn't have thought he'd care. Never mind, I shall write a nice apologetic note back, explaining how busy my leave was – when I get time.

17th October

I had a fall yesterday. All the fault of the stupid starting handle. I caught my knee a real bang with it, then crashed to the ground. My leg's really stiff today, so I'm excused cars and am to help where I can around the camp. I hobbled about, folding all the girls' thrown-off bonnet covers and stacked them beside the mess hut. I couldn't clean out the boiler (thank goodness – I hate that job) but I was able to hoe our vegetable garden until it began to rain too hard to be outside.

Someone came in with a request for a driver to take some German prisoners to hospital. I'm glad I wasn't able to. I haven't had to drive Germans yet, and I don't really want to, injured or not. Sutton says there's no need to be a fraidy-cat. You have armed guards and so on, and the prisoners are mostly not in a fit state to try it on. But still...

20th October

Today, I sang as I rinsed out my undies in a basin. Meldrew had just said, "Stow it, Rowntree!" when Jolliphant called from the window. "Hey, look!"

With that she rushed out. We followed, and saw her pick up a bird.

"Oh, poor thing!" I said. "Is it dead?"

"Afraid so," said Jolliphant. She fiddled with its leg.

"What on earth are you doing?" I demanded.

"It's a messenger pigeon," said Meldrew. "And it's carrying something. It could be vitally important."

Jolliphant took it to the Boss to be dealt with.

Messenger birds – I seem to learn something new every day. And it's not only pigeons that carry messages. Dogs do, too. And some of them are incredibly brave, dashing with their messages through areas where shells are bursting and bullets are zinging through the air. I was amazed (but not all that amazed) to find that some of those brave dogs are Airedales. I doubt if my Billie would be that brave. I wouldn't want him to be.

There's great news from Blighty. Eleven Zeppelins, sent over on a bombing raid, were destroyed. The weather had a lot to do with it, as there was a bad storm, but our anti-aircraft gunners were determined not to let them through. Hurrah!

22nd October

As if to pay us back, German planes bombed Calais during the night. We had to go out while they were still dropping their hideous loads, to rescue some of the injured and get them safely to the hospitals. It was a horrendous experience. I have never, ever been so afraid, but I'm a FANY, and fear wasn't going to stop me, or any of us, for that matter. We carried the injured, the dead and the dying amid explosions, fire and panic. For once, we didn't worry too much about gentle driving – we went for it. Thank heaven, we all returned safely.

23rd October

News from Corbett and Sutton, who've just done a comforts run. The rain at the front has been torrential, and the number of men and horses who've drowned where they fell is truly horrifying.

On their way back, they heard an aeroplane engine, but didn't see it at first, even though it was so loud. Then Corbett stuck her head out of the window and there was the aeroplane, circling right above them. And it was German.

Sutton leaned out, too, and shook her fist at the pilot. He circled once more, then flew away.

Why didn't he shoot? It can only have been because of the red crosses on the ambulance. He assumed that there were injured men inside.

I know our pilots would have done the same.

24th October

A strange, exhausting day today. We were called early this morning to do the trains. Some had to do hospital runs, and I was detailed to take my *blessés* to the boats. These were the ones who needed to be sent back to Blighty.

To be perfectly frank, I hate going down to the boats. The quay is long and so narrow that two of our ambulances can only just pass. That's OK, as long as you're not on the side nearest the water. It's a long way down, so the last thing we want to do is drive over the edge, especially with a cargo of *blessés*. It's even worse in the dark, when the rain lashes you, and the smell of the sea blends with the stink of oil.

Once our load is delivered, we drive further on to a turning place. It's not easy. You have to reverse against a platform, then there comes a point where you're at right-angles to the sea, facing it, and you have to *move forward*, inch by inch. It's impossible to see over the bonnet to gauge how close your wheels are to the edge, so it's a very tense moment. Luckily, as your vehicle's empty by then, no one can hear you swear if you do it quietly enough. One girl did go over once, but escaped out of the back of the car, thank goodness.

Anyway, today was a beast of a day, far more tiring than usual, because it was cold and foggy. I was on my last trip. The orderlies loaded up my four *blessés* on their stretchers, then asked if I could take a sitter up front with me.

"Of course," I said.

An Army captain in a filthy, torn uniform was helped in beside me. Both his hands were heavily bandaged, and his eyes looked too big for his face. I've seen that look plenty of times before. This poor man was exhausted, in a bad way, and had certainly seen the sort of sights no human being should have to witness. Apart from having his hands treated, he needed some rest and lots of comforts.

"I'm not going to the boat," he said. "They reckon a stay in hospital, with some good treatment, will put me right, then I can get back to my men. Would you be kind enough to take me there?"

How brave. I'd have been scrabbling to get on the boat back to Blighty.

We had to go slowly, of course, not just because of the fog, but because of the poor men in the back. One, who I thought looked little more than a boy when I saw him being loaded in, cried in pain, then called for his mother, which upset me terribly. But my sitter turned and spoke softly to him until he drifted into sleep. That was kind. I thought how lucky his men were to have an officer like him.

I drove as carefully as possible, but the fog made it

impossible to see the ruts and holes in the road. I desperately wanted to avoid waking the poor young boy. Far better for him to sleep the time away. I hoped he would make it home, and be able to see his mother again.

Not like Archie.

With absolutely no warning, a great sob burst from me. Oh, please, no, I thought, don't let me break down now. Not again.

The man beside me asked, "Are you all right, Miss?"

I couldn't speak. I just nodded and forced myself to think of happy things, like the concert Meldrew's planning. Then Mimi's fairies invaded my mind. I welcomed the distraction and tried to imagine what Lalu might have called her children. Peaseblossom, Cobweb and Moth, like in Shakespeare? Or names to suit their characters, like Happy, Cheeky and Lazy?

Soon I felt calm. I marvelled that Mimi's imaginary companions had helped me on this difficult journey.

I joined the line at the quay. One of the girls spotted an open *estaminet*, a little café, selling drinks and snacks, so, as we had a while to wait before we were unloaded and could be on our way, I bought a cup of tea for myself and my sitter. I also bought him a cake for ten centimes. The other *blessés*, poor souls, were beyond drinking.

I'd forgotten the captain's bandaged hands. I had to hold his cup for him as he drank, and pop bits of cake into his mouth. He was very grateful. Once, as I held the cup to his lips, I glanced up to see him looking straight into my eyes. It gave me a shiver down my spine.

Eventually my car was emptied and I drove along the quay to the turning place. I backed carefully against the platform, ready to move forward extremely cautiously towards the edge of the quay, but I overdid it! I hit the platform too hard and bounced off it – forwards!

I slammed on the brake, and we skidded to a stop. I'm sorry to say that my sitter heard me use language that would make most ladies blush.

"Sorry," I said, blushing myself.

He grinned. "I've heard worse! Well done – at least you managed to keep us out of the sea."

I pulled away, glad to be able to move at a reasonable pace. On the way to the hospital, the captain said, "My name's Charles. Charles Wensley-Croft."

"My father's name was Charles," I said. "I'm Daphne Rowntree."

When we reached the hospital an attendant checked for stretcher cases, then came round to the passenger door. But the captain said, "One moment, please," and turned to me.

"Miss Rowntree, I don't suppose you'd have time to visit me while I'm here, would you? I'm sure I shan't know another soul."

I was surprised to be asked this, but I must confess I was pleased.

"If I get time," I said.

He obviously couldn't shake hands, but he gave me a lovely tired smile as the attendant helped him out.

"Captain!"

He turned. "Charles," he reminded me.

"Charles," I said with a smile. "My friends call me Daffy."

Then I thought – actually, my friends don't call me Daffy. They call me Rowntree!

And *then* I thought: My family would be shocked to hear me being so forward with a man!

26th October

Tonight we all snuggled into our flea-bags and shouted ideas to each other for the concert.

"Meldrew's a great mimic," said Jolliphant. "She can do some impressions of well-known people."

"Rein back, Jolliphant. Nobody asked for your opinion," said Meldrew, in a perfect imitation of the Boss!

"I had a ballet mistress for seven years – seven *long* years," Sutton shouted. "I could do some sort of dance if you like."

"The dance of the seven veils!" shrieked Westerling.

"That would be ripping!" Meldrew called. "So, we have one dancer, one mimic – me – one conjuror, one trio singing

French folk songs ... and Jolliphant's doing a recitation. Anyone else volunteering?"

"Yes, me," I called. "I could sing if you like." I expected a barrage of catcalls, but none came.

It did go quiet, though. I wondered if they'd all suddenly dropped off. Then I heard a muffled, "Yes, lovely, thanks," from someone. It could have been Meldrew. I can't believe she said yes! Everyone started talking about costumes then, so I got out my book.

I'm really looking forward to the concert.

30th October

We've been so busy recently. We keep getting trainloads of victims of a dreadful new gas attack – mustard gas. The poor things are covered in painful, burning blisters, and often their eyes are swollen and gummy. Those who can speak have hoarse, whispery voices, and some become panicky because they can't breathe properly.

Today I'd finished and had lunch by three, so I offered to take a car down to the town to have a new bit welded on. I think the Boss knew I'd never remember the name of the bit, because she gave me a note to give to the mechanics.

131

I stood around waiting for a while, but got so cold that I took a brisk walk up to the nice warm hospital and asked a sister if I could see Captain Wensley-Croft. They usually let us FANYs in if at all possible.

"Of course," said the sister. "Upstairs, first left."

The captain saw me before I saw him. He was sitting on the window sill, where he'd been gazing out at the murky day. "How perfectly good of you to come," he said.

"That's all right," I told him. "I was passing anyway."

"Oh."

"So how are you?" I asked brightly. "The bandages look a little smaller – and a lot cleaner."

He laughed. "I'm fine. Just itching to get out of here."

We talked for a while, and when he was brought a cup of tea I helped him drink it.

"Just like old times," he said, and smiled his lovely smile.

Then I asked, "If I come again, would you like to go outside for a stroll, if they'll let you? I'm sure if you wrapped up warm they'd—"

"Daffy, I'd love to."

He's really very nice.

31st October

A German ship – a destroyer – fired shells into Calais tonight! More than 100. Maybe 200. We got one, right behind the cookhouse. Spent hours clearing up and getting over the shock. All I've had today is hot soup.

1st November

The army's battling for control of a village called Passchendaele, which will help them in their push forward to the Belgian coast, so they can attack the German submarine bases. They've got troops from our allies with them at Passchendaele, too: Australians, New Zealanders, South Africans, Canadians and so on. It'll soon be ours!

Of course, the bigger the battle, the more casualties there are, and we've been working like billy-o. I did a long session on barges today. It was hellish getting up early after little more than an hour's sleep. My first load were all destined for the hospital, and the orderly who saw them into my ambulance confided in me that not one of the four is expected to make it.

It's terribly upsetting. I was miserable for the whole of the rest of the day. I've been doing this for quite a while now, and I shouldn't let it get to me. But under every brown blanket is a man – sometimes just a boy – who is loved by someone else. And on every small brown pillow is a face that a mother or brother or wife or sweetheart longs to see. Sometimes the poor faces are so damaged they won't be recognized – that's all part of the horror of this filthy war.

It was lovely to get back to camp to find the post had been delivered. I saved mine until after supper, so I could read it in peace and quiet, but I'd reckoned without Meldrew practising her impressions of people. It was quite unnerving hearing voices I recognized!

A sweet letter from Reggie (nothing from Elizabeth Baguley, I notice). He said he misses seeing me when he's riding out, but has called on my mother and she is well, though busy. Bless him, he checked on Honeycomb, too, and says she's looking fit and healthy, and Hawkins exercises her regularly. Billie just stuck his nose in the air and ignored Reggie. Reggie, sensibly, ignored Gulliver.

I said it was a sweet letter, and it was, so far. Reggie went on to say he quite understands me joining the FANY, and doesn't think any the less of me for it.

I was so incensed by that last bit that I read it out to the other girls. Instead of getting annoyed, like me, they just hooted with laughter, and said they'd like to see that idiot doing barges at four o'clock on an icy winter morning – with no lights and no moon.

I can imagine what Reggie will think of my hair.

4th November

There were no ambulance calls this morning, so at ten to eight the whistle went for parade and roll call, and then we settled down for a peaceful brekker. We have a French woman coming in to help now. She's very willing, but she suffers from dropsy. Not the ailment known as dropsy – she just drops everything. I had to go outside to get my car shipshape with the stain from a whole fried egg on my polished leather boot.

For once everything went right with my daily motor maintenance, then, before cleaning the car inside and out, two of us tidied our hut. I was hoping there'd be a call for someone to go down to the hospital, or at least near it, but nothing came. Then at nearly four o'clock, in the middle of a heavy hailstorm, an Army car screeched into camp, and a soldier jumped out.

"Post for anyone as wants it," he yelled, waving a bundle in the air. He made a dash for cover, but slipped and fell to his knees. The idiot dropped all our mail and down it sploshed into an icy puddle.

There were cries of fury as the girls rushed out to rescue their precious letters and packages. I didn't go. It wasn't that I minded getting wet. I just felt so cross. I'd have liked to have gone down to the quay for the mail. I'd have liked to see Captain Wensley-Croft again.

Jolliphant saw my long face when she bounced back. "Letters for you, Rowntree – hey, what's wrong? You look pale. Are you lovesick or something?"

Am I?

7th November

Wonderful news. The village of Passchendaele is ours! This means that the Germans are on the losing end and, soon, so will their U-boats be – we hope.

We've all managed to get hold of gloriously warm fur coats. Some are goat, some are wolf, and some are most peculiar. I sent for mine from home, and it feels most odd to be wearing it in the middle of the night, in France, in the pitch black. They're not proper uniform, but everyone turns a blind eye because driving without a windscreen is perishingly cold. We couldn't do it if we didn't have warm clothing.

Tonight a group of us went out to dinner in the town, to celebrate Passchendaele. Afterwards, we found a dance and wheedled our way in. We had the jolliest time imaginable, but kept our coats with us all the time – it would never do to have those stolen, not now winter's here. It's freezing at night, waiting in line for trains or barges.

8th November

I volunteered to take some broken engine parts down to the mechanics this morning, so I could slip in to the hospital.

"How are you, Captain?" I asked.

He smiled. "I told you before, it's Charles."

"Charles," I said with a nod. "I can't stop – I just wanted to see how you were."

He held up his hands. "I've had my bandages off all morning, but they put thick goo all over my hands, so I'm strapped up again. Mustn't dirty the sheets, or I'll have Sister after me." He glanced over my shoulder and winked. "Won't I, Sister?"

I turned to see a pretty red-headed nurse smiling at him. I smiled, too, but inside I silently wished she'd go away. She must have got the message, because she did.

"I'll be back as soon as I can," I said, and gripped his wrist instead of shaking hands.

He looked down. "I wish I could hold your hand, Daffy. Maybe one day soon?"

"Goodbye," I said.

As I left, my own hands were shaking. When I got into the car, I noticed that, as usual, my nails were lined with black oil. What must he have thought?

Later

When I got back, the Boss said, "Where the deuce have you been, Rowntree? There's a job for you."

She gave me an address and told me I was to pick up some German prisoners and take them to a hospital about thirty kilometres away.

"Yes, Boss," I said, but she must have seen the expression on my face. I did *not* want to do it.

"Rowntree," she said. "Do you remember the FANY motto?"

"Yes, Boss," I said proudly. "It's '*Arduis invictus*'."

"And what does it mean?"

That was a difficult one. I'd never bothered to find out. "Er, something about unconquered, and, er, *arduis* – let me see. Something hard?"

"Unconquered in hardship!" The Boss glared at me. "And that means what?"

"Er, that means..."

"It means you cope!" she snapped. "You may not like the job I'm giving you – your face made that perfectly clear – but you jolly well get on and do it!"

I felt *awful*.

I picked up the prisoners – there were only two and I had an armed guard with me. Both Germans had shaven heads and really shabby uniforms. They actually looked to be in quite a bad way. One had his eyes open, but his face was flushed and his breathing was shallow. I hope he didn't have typhoid. I've had my typhoid jab – we all have – and I gargle like mad to keep my throat clear of germs, but it doesn't do to take chances. The other man was out cold. His forehead was bandaged and there was blood where his ear was – at least I hope his ear was there.

The guard was one of those absolute blighters who talk non-stop about themselves, but never ask you any questions about yourself. If I ventured anything like, "We've been very busy lately," then he'd been busier. Or if I said, "We're planning a concert," he'd once put on a gala performance. I had a wicked impulse to tell him I'd got a new lace petticoat, just to see what he'd come out with!

After a while he exhausted himself and fell asleep. I drove along in silence. I must admit I wasn't quite so careful with holes in the road as I would have been if they were our British Tommies in the back.

We were nearly at the hospital, and I was just congratulating myself for coping (yes, Boss, I remembered) with my first encounter with the enemy, when there was a movement behind me. I glanced round to see the man with the bandaged head sitting bolt upright, eyes wide, staring.

He suddenly spouted a load of German. I don't know if he was cursing me or not, but I don't think he was being complimentary. I dug my elbow into the guard. "Wake up!"

"Eh? Wassup?" he spluttered.

I jerked a thumb over my shoulder. "Him."

"What?"

Looking swiftly over my shoulder I saw that the man was lying down again.

The guard gave me a look, as if to say, "Women!"

I was livid. Who'd have thought I'd end my first go at driving prisoners by disliking the guard more than the Germans?

9th November

Last night, lying on my bed, I relived that trip. It struck me that the Germans were no different from any of our regular *blessés*. They were injured men. Somebody's son. Somebody's brother.

Oh, Papa! Oh, Archie! I cried myself to sleep.

11th November

Sutton and I took supplies up to the front yesterday. It seems so civilized here compared to what we find as we travel. Each time I've done this trip, or one like it, it's been foul weather, and yesterday was no exception. It's rained or sleeted almost non-stop for three days now, and the mud just gets worse and worse. We passed a woman walking with a child in ragged clothes. They stopped and waved, and the child's little wet face shone when she smiled. I thought of my sister May. As we drove through villages, dogs barked at us. They were so thin and neglected. I wish I could take them all home.

Whenever we pass Tommies walking back from the front to their well-earned rest, you can hardly believe they'll ever get clean. Their boots and legs are absolutely caked and it's not with dry mud – it's wet. Even though the rain and wind blast on to my face, freezing my cheeks, I am so glad that I have my car to get about in.

We were carrying a bumper load of knitted goods, so we slithered to a stop and doled out socks and mufflers and other goodies whenever we could. The men were so grateful. One said he only possessed one sock and that had rotted into holes. "I used the other one to clean out me rifle," he said, "then I put it down and some blighter pinched it."

Poor brave souls.

Sutton has a brother in the Army. She says the trenches stink and there's absolutely nowhere dry. Every time it rains, the trenches flood again, and the men have to put up with it, wearing the same clothes day and night. They make dugouts, and huddle in them when they're off watch, trying to keep warm. They take bundles of straw down in the trenches, to sit on, but the straw ends up being home for vermin. Ugh.

I felt so pleased with myself because Sutton talked about her brother, and I didn't go on about Archie, and I didn't cry. Oh dear, I spoke too soon. Now the tears are leaking.

13th November

A full train day today. I did three complete runs with stretcher cases, then one load of sitters. After that we went back, picked up the stretcher-bearers and returned them to their camp. All I had to do after that was drop off a package of mail at the quay and then I was free. I told the other girls I'd be late for supper, and cut across to Charles's hospital.

He was delighted to see me. We chatted for a few moments, and I told him I could allow myself about half an hour before whizzing down to drop the mail off at the boat.

The ward sister very kindly gave me a cup of tea when she brought Charles's. It seemed so cosy, drinking tea together. He was even able to hold his cup if I put it between his bandaged hands.

All too soon it was time to go. As I left the ward, I thanked the sister for the tea and she said, "Are you going near the quay?"

"Yes," I said. "I'm delivering mail."

"Perfect," she said. "Could you take my patients' letters and postcards, please? They'll get back to Blighty that much more quickly than if we wait until tomorrow."

I took the mail gladly. Once down near the quay, I joined a queue, and sat wondering whether to park and continue on foot, or just wait my turn.

Quicker to walk, I decided, and reached for the FANY post. I scooped up the hospital mail, and a couple of postcards slipped off. As I picked them up, I saw one was signed with a scrawled "Charles". My Charles is the only one in the ward, and as the handwriting was very feminine, it had to be his. He would have got one of the nurses to write it for him.

As someone else had written the card, I reasoned, it wasn't exactly private. I squinted at it. *Dear Mother*, it began.

Had he mentioned me? I wondered. And then I did a stupid thing, though looking back, I'm glad I did it. I read the card.

Dear Mother,

If this reaches you safely, you'll know that I'm nearly well. I should rejoin my regiment soon, but I won't be at the front line for a while, so don't worry about me. I'm so relieved that Mabel has left London, but as I'm stuck down here in Calais, her letters haven't reached me, and I don't yet have her new address. Please drop her a line on my behalf – tell her I miss her terribly, that I love her with all my heart, and cannot wait for us to be together again.

As the signature was scrawly, I assumed he'd had a stab at signing it himself. He might as well have stabbed my heart.

I don't remember any more until I got back to camp. I must have delivered the mail because it wasn't on the seat beside me when I returned.

I thought I'd found someone – someone who really cared for me. Not the me who wears hats and gloves and goes to tea with Elizabeth Baguley. Not the me who helps Mimi run the household. The *real* me.

But he loves Mabel. His fiancée? His *wife*? Either way, he should have told me. He shouldn't have pretended to care for me. That wasn't fair.

Jolliphant found me hiding in the cookhouse, snivelling in the dark over a plate of bread and jam. I told her. I told her all of it.

"Maybe he wasn't pretending," she said. "I suppose it might be possible to care for two people at once. I know I care for all our horses."

That was true. I think I love Archie and Honeycomb both the same. But no! "This is different," I said. "He's married or, at the very least, engaged, and he's been betraying his wife as well as – as..."

"As well as leading you up the garden path," said Jolliphant. "The blighter. Come on, Rowntree, everyone's practising for the concert, and we haven't heard your song yet."

"I don't feel like singing." But I got up and followed her.

The girls were awfully nice and pretended not to notice my pink eyes and bunged-up nose.

Later

When the temperature drops below freezing, we have to take turns to sit up at night and start the motor engines every hour to warm them up. Otherwise they freeze, and they're impossible to start in the mornings. We can't have that. When a FANY's needed, she has to be ready. It's my watch at the moment. I hate it. One minute I'm warm in my flea-bag, the next I'm out in this freezing weather struggling with starting handles. And I have too much time to think. I keep remembering poor Violet's misery when Archie went missing. My thoughts towards her weren't exactly charitable. I feel bad about that now.

14th November

I feel better today. Last night's practice certainly took my mind off my sorrows. Meldrew was hilarious, and Jolliphant recited a poem she'd written herself. The last line of each verse was the same, and we were told to join in on that line, so the audience would join in, too.

"It's good to get the audience participating," said Meldrew. "They'll enjoy themselves so much more if they feel they're part of the occasion."

Sutton is a dark horse. She must have spent hours in secret making a beautiful Arabian costume. Her performance was a mixture of Eastern dance movements and ballet, and was just the most beautiful thing I've ever seen. How could she be so light on her feet? I suppose I've only ever seen her in boots.

Then it was my turn. I had to sing unaccompanied, of course, as we've no piano here. I began, and almost instantly, there was a hush. Once I'd finished, I closed my eyes for a moment, and laid a graceful hand across my chest, as I've seen professional singers do.

I opened my eyes to find everyone staring at me.

"That was – amazing," said Meldrew.

Everyone nodded furiously. "Amazing. Absolutely amazing!"

Bless them, they're so polite! I really must stop fooling about and tell them I know I'm not much of a singer.

16th November

Today I was collecting laundry in the town when I noticed a group of French people staring up at the sky and pointing. It was an aeroplane, a German one, they shouted, and it was in trouble. It fell for a few seconds like a sycamore wing, then plummeted, nose down, fast. The locals told me the pilot had probably been shot; they could see him clearly, slumped across the front of the aeroplane. I know he was the enemy, but I wouldn't wish anyone to end up in crumpled wreckage in a foreign land.

18th November

The concert was last night. I'm glad it was, as I had such an upsetting day. I was at the canal quay this morning, and when they loaded my *blessés*, one of them tried to grasp my hand, but his grip was too weak. I smoothed the hair from his forehead and he whispered, "Pocket." Oh, gosh, it brings a lump to my throat just to write about it.

What happened was that he asked me to find a photo, and I was surprised when I saw it, since it was of himself. He begged me to send it to his mother, and I said, "You'll be able to send it yourself when you're better."

But when we arrived at the hospital, the poor boy was dead. I was the last person to speak to him and I didn't even know his name. The attendant who came with me promised he would see that the photo reaches the boy's mother, and I believe him.

So what a relief it was to get back and find concert preparations in full swing. We held it in a huge Army tent. Jolliphant was worried there wouldn't be enough room for the audience, but Meldrew said, "If there isn't, we shall just do the whole thing twice." She and Sutton had somehow produced some shiny yellow curtains, and one of the mechanics had rigged up some very decent lighting.

I was on the point of telling them I didn't expect to sing, when I heard Meldrew saying how brilliant it was that every single one of us was having a go, even though we were all complete amateurs. And I thought, why shouldn't I have a go? I only hoped I wouldn't get booed off.

We'd just got to the stage when we thought no one was coming, when the first of the Tommies wandered in. He was followed by more soldiers, a few Navy men, and quite a number of nurses and sisters from the various hospitals round about. There was even a smattering of French people, some of whom looked as if they were daring you to make them smile.

I was due to go on first after the interval, and I was jolly nervous. But then Meldrew came over and whispered to me, "Sutton says she'll be sick if she doesn't get her act over and done with soon. Would you mind awfully giving her your slot after the interval?"

"No, of course I don't mind, but what about—"

"Actually, we wanted to ask you a huge favour. We've

decided it would be fun to have a sing-song at the end, for the audience to join in, and it would be a really big finish, don't you think?"

"Well, yes," I said, "but—"

"So what we wondered was this," said Meldrew hurriedly. "Would you be a bird and, instead of just doing your one song, lead the whole sing-song for us, get all the audience on their feet, singing their hearts out? It would be so good for morale."

"Gosh!" I said. "That's very flattering."

"Oh, please say yes," begged Meldrew. "None of us has a voice as, well, as *big* as yours. We'd never be heard, but you would."

I smiled. "Of course."

She looked awfully relieved as she went off and got into a huddle with some of the other girls. I hastily gathered together a list of songs that everybody would know, and soon it was my turn.

I hesitate to say that it was a triumph, but from the minute I opened my mouth, the combined voices practically lifted the tent into the air! The girls were, of course, ranged behind me, and they sang their hearts out from the start.

Halfway through, I looked at all the faces in front of me and thought, if only Archie was among them. I still haven't rid myself of the habit of scanning every soldier's face I pass. I don't suppose I ever will.

We girls all got into our nightclothes afterwards and celebrated with two bottles of French wine that one of the officers gave us. It was rather sharp, but fun to drink.

I slept well. The last thing I remember was vowing to myself that tomorrow I would go down to the hospital, speak to Charles, and be perfectly plain about my feelings. Then I would say goodbye.

But now it's early morning. I'm lying in my flea-bag writing this, my mouth tastes yellow and I don't feel like doing that at all.

Maybe I had too much wine.

20th November

My sponge was frozen this morning, and I had to thaw it over the oil stove. And I swear there was ice on my pillow, where my breath had frozen. Oh, I hate this weather. My hands feel raw all the time I'm driving.

Thankfully, four of us had a break from barges and trains today, so we set about cleaning the hut. It goes for days without a proper clean-out. Honeycomb wouldn't stand for such squalor! I worked slowly, and I think I was putting off the moment when I'd have to face Charles and tell him exactly how I felt. Then I knocked over the clothes horse and had to re-wash everybody's undies.

So, one way and another, I didn't get a chance to go down to see him until teatime this afternoon.

And he's gone.

The ward sister said Captain Wensley-Croft was well enough to rejoin his regiment, though he won't be firing a gun for quite a while.

He left me a note. I took it back to my car to read. It said:

Dearest Daffy,

I've looked for you every day. I'm so sad not to see you, just as we're becoming close. We are becoming close, aren't we? And now I must leave without saying goodbye – or rather, au revoir.

As soon as I can, I will come back and see you. I hope we can pick up our friendship where we left off.

Your affectionate

Charles

Your affectionate Charles, indeed! He's not mine. He's Mabel's. And she's welcome to him. I wouldn't want a man who would betray anyone, let alone a wife. Or fiancée – or even a sweetheart – it's all the same.

30th November

What do I remember?

At first, all I could remember was waking up here in the hospital. But it's coming back to me.

My leg hurts. They tell me I was shot, but I can't remember that. The nurses give me medicine to help the pain, but it never goes completely. I do what I can to take my mind off it. I can't walk, of course, not yet. But I can read. I even played a game of cards with Jolliphant, who comes to see me whenever she can. Several of the girls have been. They don't stay long. I get tired.

Later

Even writing tires me. The doctor says it's probably shock.

What do I remember?

I remember Westerling and I driving a car each down into Calais late one afternoon. We collected mountains of Red Cross supplies – the stretcher spaces were packed tight. I took a passenger – a Red Cross man, Eric, who was going up to one of the casualty clearing stations near the front to distribute all the stuff. I didn't envy him. We'd had nothing but rain for several days before, and it had suddenly turned bitterly cold and the roads were treacherous with patchy ice. Driving conditions were atrocious, and I knew the conditions at the front must be horrendous. I had never been so glad of my fur coat.

The sky darkened earlier than usual.

"A rainstorm's on its way," said Eric, his voice sounding muffled because of the big scarf he'd wrapped round his neck and face.

I couldn't reply, because my lips were numb.

The weather worsened, and it was soon clear that we were heading right into the worst of it. One good thing was that more rain would mean the ice on the roads would melt.

I remember little of the journey except the bleakness of the landscape. Oh yes, I remember the level crossing, and Sleepy Suzanne ignoring my hooter. Eric jumped out and lifted the barriers, which meant Westerling had to close them again.

Nearer the front everything was dead or dying. Shelled houses crumbled and decayed, almost before your eyes. There was no sign of life. Even the chickens we sometimes saw scratching around must have been sheltering where they could. Perhaps they'd been caught and eaten. There were no scavenging dogs or cats. The burned and shattered trees stood like stalagmites, pointing towards the blackening sky, where there wasn't a bird to be seen. In the distance, flashes and flames and the constant booming of the guns guided us to our destination.

I remember passing a ruined farmhouse, and in the little blasted orchard beside it, three white-painted crosses gleamed in the darkness. I remember hooded figures unloading the Red Cross supplies and I remember saying goodbye to Eric against a background of explosions. I remember having my first experience of hearing a shell really close to, and both hearing and seeing the explosion. Thank heaven it landed in empty ground.

Westerling ran over to me, holding her coat above her head. "Let's get out of here!" she cried.

I couldn't have agreed more. I ran round to the driver's door and screamed as something hit me hard in the face. It was hail. And not ordinary hail – these were lumps of ice, some as big as gooseberries.

I pulled in behind Westerling and we set off. I was determined to stay close to her – it wouldn't do to get separated or, worse, stranded in those conditions. Our cars slithered as we struggled to get a tyre-hold in the mud and icy slush, and the hail drove straight into my face, stinging me. It was going to be a hellish journey home.

1st December

Now I remember. I remember an officer standing on the side of the road. His car had gone off into a ditch and was well and truly embedded in mud. The front wheels had all but disappeared. We slowed, he exchanged a few words with Westerling, then climbed into her car.

Thankfully, the hail turned to sleety rain, but once darkness had truly fallen I had a struggle to keep sight of the car in front. Westerling had her own problems, as she was very much the pathfinder. Visibility must have been even worse for her. I didn't expect her to keep checking to see if I was behind. It was up to me to keep up.

After a few kilometres the cloud began to break up a little, and on a couple of occasions I briefly glimpsed the moon. The rain eased, and the outline of Westerling's vehicle in front became more visible. We still had to wrestle to stay on the road, though, as it was awash with mud and all sorts of debris.

We drove down into a dip, crossed a swollen stream or ditch and, as we climbed the slope on the other side I suddenly saw something – an animal – moving, just off to the right, in front. It all happened at once.

"Billie!" I screamed, but of course it wasn't. It *was* an Airedale though, and the poor thing was dragging a hind leg. Almost at the moment I realized what it was, my foot slammed on the brake. The car slithered to the edge of the road and first one front wheel slipped over, then the other. For once I was grateful that I didn't have a proper windscreen, because I would have gone through it, head first. As it was I nearly went out the front over the bonnet.

I forced the door open and jumped out, up to my knees in foul-smelling sloppy mud, which oozed over the tops of my boots. Slipping and sliding, I climbed back on to the road and ran to the dog.

"Hey there, old chap," I said gently. "You're hurt, aren't you? Scared, too," I added, as the boom-boom-boom of the guns suddenly seemed louder than ever. "Never mind, I've got an ambulance. I'll take care of you."

Airedales are too big to carry, so I helped the poor creature along the road, back towards the car. Westerling had driven on. She obviously hadn't noticed I'd stopped. I was alone. I looked around. Darkness was everywhere. I couldn't see a single light anywhere. Not a glimmer.

I stopped every couple of steps, to give the poor, soaking wet dog a rest. As we finally neared the car I became aware of movement on my right and heard the sound of panting. My heart tumbled over.

"*Aus dem Wege!*" said a deep voice. "Out of the way! Move, please!"

A German. I was face to face with a German. "The dog," I squeaked. "He's hurt. I just want to—"

He raised a gun. "Move! *Lass den Hund!* Leave the dog!"

"Please," I begged. "*Bitte?*" Why hadn't I bothered to learn a few words of German? But it didn't matter. He had enough English to make me understand.

"The dog. *Er muss sterben.* It must die. You will please move. *Move!*"

I don't know why I did it. I'm not brave. Maybe I thought of Billie, although there was hardly time. But I couldn't let him kill the poor animal in cold blood. He would kill me anyway, so it didn't matter. As he raised the gun to fire, I threw myself in front of the dog.

There was a flash and a brain-bursting explosion, and something thumped me in the knee. Moments later came excruciating pain, then ... nothing.

2nd December

I feel better today. The pain is easing, but I'm told it will be a long time before my leg is better. At least I remember how I came to be shot. I still can't believe it. Someone must have written to Mimi, because I've had a very sorrowful letter from her, all about how I promised I wouldn't drive into danger. She didn't mention being shot, so I think she's been spared the details. How will she feel when she knows what really happened? That I was shot trying to save a dog. Not a very noble deed, I suppose, in these dreadful times when men and boys are being killed in their thousands or, like Archie, just disappearing.

4th December

Gosh. I've had an unexpected visitor. Westerling, who I last saw disappearing into the rainy blackness, came to see me, and brought an Army officer with her. At first I thought she must have found herself a sweetheart, but then she introduced him to me. He was the officer she picked up that dreadful night, after we left the casualty clearing station. He asked us to call him Nigel, and he's very sweet, in an old-fashioned sort of way. Rather like my papa, in fact.

"Rowntree, you were incredibly brave," Westerling said, shoving a paper bag of jam tarts into my hand. "We're all so desperately proud of you." She sat in a chair beside my bed.

"It didn't take much bravery to get shot," I said. "I didn't know it was coming and, to be frank, if I'd known how much it would hurt, I'd definitely have run the other way."

Nigel smiled. "I'm glad you didn't. May I?" He patted the bed.

I nodded and he sat down. Instantly, the ward sister beetled across and said, "No sitting on beds."

Nigel leapt up. "Sorry! Sorry, Sister!"

It always amazes me that these officers put themselves in front of German shells and bullets and bombs every day, yet they're terrified by a nurse.

"I'll fetch you a chair if you need to sit," she said, smoothing my bedspread.

"No, no thank you," said Nigel. "We won't be here long."

"That's right," said the sister.

Nigel relaxed once she'd left the ward. I offered him a jam tart, then caught Westerling's eye. She was trying hard not to laugh at him.

"So what happened that night?" I asked. "I still don't know how I got here. What did you do when you got back and discovered I was missing?"

"We didn't," she said. "When we set off, I could hardly see anything in front of me, and I was terrified of driving into a shell hole, or going off the road nose down into a canal or ditch. So I told Nigel I'd concentrate on the road, if he kept checking to see that you were behind us. There came a point when he said you'd disappeared."

"So Miss Westerling slowed down, and I was to let her know when you caught up," said Nigel, helping himself to a second jam tart. I took a bite of mine. It was delicious.

"And of course, you didn't catch up," continued Westerling. "So I did about a 23-point turn—"

"Thank goodness for all that practice on the Calais quay," I said. "What then?"

The ward sister bustled in with a chair. "Sit down, please," she said to Nigel. "You make the room look untidy."

"Then," said Westerling, "then came the exciting bit. Thanks to the dreadful weather and the racket from the front, not to mention star shells exploding in the sky, your German didn't notice us coming until we were almost upon him. Nigel here, who's an absolute hero, leapt out while we were still moving, and knocked him to the ground! He banged the German's arm again and again until he dropped the gun and, in seconds, it was all over. I, of course, was attending to you, and when I turned round, I found I had a trussed-up German prisoner in the back of my dear little ambulance!"

"And me?"

"I'm afraid you were put in the back above him," said Nigel. "If you'd opened your eyes, we didn't want the first person you saw to be the man who'd just shot you!"

Westerling laughed. "You'll be pleased to know you bled on him."

I laughed, too, for the first time since I woke in hospital.

Unfortunately I spluttered crumbs on the bedsheets. Sister would be cross about that. Maybe I could sweeten her up with a tart or two.

"I think that's everything," said Westerling.

"The dog? What about the dog? Did someone take care of it?"

They both smiled. "We brought the dog back in the ambulance." Westerling looked at Nigel. "We had to, didn't we?"

Nigel nodded. "You see, Miss Rowntree, when I said I was glad you hadn't run the other way, it doesn't mean I was glad you got shot. I was glad you didn't leave the dog to the German."

I smiled. "Poor thing. How could I? I've got an Airedale exactly like him at home."

A lump came into my throat as I thought of home, and Mimi, Freddie and May, and of Honeycomb and Billie and even Gulliver.

"Nigel," I said. "My brother, Archibald Rowntree, he's—"

"Yes, Miss Westerling told me. I'll do all I can, Miss Rowntree, but I have to tell you that it's most unlikely—"

"I know." I pulled the blankets up to my chin. "Actually, I think I'd like to rest now. Thank you for coming to visit me. And – thank you for saving my life."

Nigel rose and looked down at me seriously. "You haven't let me finish telling you about the dog. He wasn't an ordinary dog. He was a messenger dog." He crouched down so his face was level with mine. "Your Airedale was carrying a message, and if that message hadn't got through, many, many lives would have been lost."

I didn't trust myself to speak. Westerling smoothed my hair back. "You thanked us for saving your life, Rowntree, but the truth is, you've saved many more."

I began to sob. I don't know what's the matter with me, I truly don't.

"The Airedale will go back to work, Miss Rowntree," said Nigel.

Westerling took my hand. "But you have to go home."

Later

So that's it. I'm for Blighty. I never found Archie. Not that I was really looking for him – not exactly. I suppose, in my ignorance, and Mimi's, I thought all I had to do was turn up in Calais and ask, "Has anybody here seen Archie?"

5th December

I'm to leave on the boat tomorrow. Jolliphant brought me a postcard from Charles. It said he hopes to be back in this area in a few days, and would like to see me. Unless he comes in the next 24 hours, he's had it. And I don't care.

Except that I do care, very much. But I must put Charles out of my mind. He belongs to someone else.

6th December

I'm so touched. All the girls came down to say goodbye today. There was a nice sister on duty, and she and the nurses turned a blind eye to the noisy crowd around my bed.

"Everyone wanted to drive you to the quay, Rowntree," said Meldrew. "So we raffled you off."

"Who won?"

"Westerling," said Jolliphant. "And it sort of fits, as she's the only one who's driven you since you were shot."

In the end, Meldrew, Jolliphant and a couple of others squeezed in with me, and off we went.

I wept buckets when I was carried on board. I wept for my friends, for Archie, for Papa, for the Airedale and, most of all, for myself. I was leaving one place where I truly felt I belonged, where people liked me for who I am, and didn't expect me to be what I am not.

And I was leaving Charles behind. I know he's not for me, but I shed a tear for what might have been.

13th December

Four ghastly, dreary days in hospital, and at last I'm home. Elsie says she's missed me terribly, but that might have something to do with the fact that she's had to help the housemaids while I've been away. Freddie and May keep coming up to my room to read to me, which is lovely, but wearing.

Mimi seems well. Aunt Eloise says she doesn't talk about the fairies unless someone asks her about them. "And only that fool of a maid of hers does that," said Aunt Eloise.

The first thing Mimi said, after hugging me as if she would never let me go, was, "Whatever happened to your hair?"

"I had it cut."

"On purpose?" said Aunt Eloise.

"Yes," I said, unwilling to tell them I'd been set upon! "D'you like it?"

After a brief pause, Aunt Eloise spoke first. "Actually I do. It must save a lot of time in the mornings."

"I think it's very nice, darling," said Mimi. She was lying.

Uncle Cecil says Mr Boone is managing the estate in an appropriate manner. He and Aunt Leonora are very proud of me, he says. But he suggests I grow my hair.

Bobby's coming to see me this afternoon. I'm looking forward to that. In the meantime, I'm just lying on the sofa in my bedroom. It's a bit of a squash because Billie's up here with me. He's such a comfort. I don't want to let him go!

Later

The first thing Bobby said was, "I like the hair!" Then she wanted to hear every detail about my "accident", and said she was going to tell all her chums about her brave cousin.

It's odd. Here I am, laid out with a bullet hole in my leg and, apart from Bobby, all people talk about is my hair.

14th December

Elsie brought the post up to me this morning. There was a letter from Charles, forwarded by the FANY office. I opened it. It was very brief, just saying that he was terribly sorry to hear of my accident, that he misses me, and that he would like to visit me when he's back in England. Which, he hopes, won't be too long.

How can he keep on like this? His Mabel knows nothing of this, so it cannot be hurting her. But it hurts me badly. I threw the letter away. I don't expect to hear any more from him.

16th December

Elsie brought another letter from Charles, but I told her to burn it.

"Are you sure, Miss Daphne?"

"I'm sure. Study the handwriting, Elsie, and if any more readdressed letters come in the same writing, destroy them."

"Yes, Miss."

17th December

Oh, I do wish Bobby had been here this afternoon! Lady Baguley and Elizabeth called to see me. They were so sweet. They brought flowers, a pretty bottle of rosewater and two beautifully embroidered handkerchiefs. Elizabeth's work, of course.

We talked for almost an hour. Lady Baguley could hardly believe some of the things I've done. "An engine!" she said in amazement. "You cleaned an engine? But wasn't it terribly dirty?"

I was very good. I didn't laugh.

Elizabeth was absolutely riveted by my exploits, especially my tale of the German who shot me.

I kept catching Lady Baguley staring at me, but she is too well-bred to mention my hair. However, as they were leaving, Elizabeth kissed my cheek and whispered. "I think you look very nice, Daphne. Very – very modern."

As her mother went downstairs, Elizabeth popped her

head back in and said, "I forgot. Reggie would like to call on you. May he?"

She didn't forget. She just didn't want her mother to know that Reggie wants to see me. It wouldn't do to have her nephew paying his attentions to a tomboy like me. I shrugged. "I suppose so."

Elizabeth looked taken aback by my ungracious reply. Oh dear, Daffy – that might be how a FANY speaks, but it's not how to speak to a Baguley.

20th December

What a day. Oh, what a day.

I was lying on my bedroom sofa with Billie beside me, watching the snow falling on the mulberry tree, when Elsie burst into the room. She pulled herself up straight and knocked. A bit late when she was already over the threshold!

"Oh, Miss Daphne!"

"Yes, Elsie, what is it?" I said calmly, thinking she'd probably broken my soap dish or scorched one of my dresses – again.

"It's a gentleman, Miss. Oh, what's his name? Is it Wednesday?"

"No, it's Thursday, Elsie. Now try to remember the name. Is it Mr Reginald Baguley?"

"No, Miss." She scratched her head, pulling a clump of hair loose from her cap. "Oh, I've got it. Wednesday-Croft. Yes," she said, pleased with herself. "That's his name."

Charles. My heart leapt, and I felt thrilled and sick, both at the same time.

"Shall I bring him up, Miss Daphne?"

"Yes. No. Oh, I suppose I must see him if he's come all this way." I grabbed my hand mirror. "Elsie, is my hair neat? Is my blouse crumpled? Oh, I hate not being able to walk properly!"

"You look perfect, Miss Daphne," said Elsie. She tweaked my hair and stood back, satisfied.

"Then please fetch the gentleman."

"Yes, Miss." She bobbed a curtsey and left, closing the door behind her.

I remembered what we were told to do in first aid if we felt queasy or nervous, and took some deep steadying breaths. Unfortunately, they just made me feel light-headed.

There was a tap on the door, and Elsie entered.

"Captain Wednesday-Croft," she announced, standing aside to let him pass.

"Good morning, Captain," I said coolly.

"Daffy." He gazed down at me. I heard Elsie close the door quietly. "How are you?"

"I'm well, thank you, apart from – you know." I gestured at my leg.

"Of course. I was so sorry to hear—"

I didn't want to hear how sorry he was, so I interrupted. "Do sit down."

"Thank you. Did you receive my letters?" he asked.

"Yes, I did."

He shuffled his feet. "You didn't answer them."

I stroked Billie's head and said nothing.

"He's a fine dog." Charles watched Billie for a few moments, then looked up. "Daffy, I've had the devil of a job finding you. The FANY women wouldn't give me your address. They said if I wrote care of their office in Earl's Court Road, my letters would be forwarded."

I didn't know what to say, so I said, "Yes, they're very efficient."

"But you didn't reply, so I thought perhaps the FANY people had ditched them. Now that I know you received them, I don't know what to say."

That made two of us, but I've always believed honesty is the best policy. I took a deep breath and said, "I didn't reply to your letters, because it would not have been appropriate to do so." I quite surprised myself when I said that – I sounded just like Lady Baguley!

"Not appropriate?" he said. "Daffy, you surely know that I care for you. I care deeply for you. And I'd begun to hope that you cared for me, too."

It was too much. I sat bolt upright. "How can I care for you?" I burst out. "And how dare you say you care for me when you already love someone else?"

"Someone else!" He leaned forward. "What are you talking about?"

"Your wife," I snapped. "Or your fiancée, or sweetheart or whatever she is!" I felt a moment's uneasiness when I saw how bewildered he looked.

"She?" he said. "Who the devil are you talking about?"

"Mabel! That's who! I apologize for reading your postcard, but I did and there it is." He went to speak, but I carried on. "And I'm glad I did."

I sank back on my cushions. Charles, too, sat back.

"Mabel," he said. "I see. You read my postcard."

I kept quiet.

Charles felt around in his pocket and brought out a leather wallet. He took a photograph from it, which he held towards me. "Daffy," he said. "This is Mabel."

I turned my head away, but he held the photograph in front of my face so I couldn't help but look. (I would have done, anyway, because I was curious.)

What I saw took my breath away.

"This is Mabel?" I asked.

He nodded.

"She's beautiful," I said. It was true. She was the prettiest little girl I've ever seen.

"She's eight years old, and she's my sister," said Charles.

As I went to speak he held up a hand. "When she was two, Mabel nearly drowned. There was no one else around but me. I pulled her out of the water and as I fought to bring her back to life, I vowed that if she lived, I would always look after her. We love each other dearly."

"Oh." I truly didn't know what to say.

Just then there was a gentle tapping at the door and Mimi came in. She looked apprehensive. I introduced her and she said to Charles, "I heard you were here, Captain. Have you come with news of my son?"

"I'm sorry, Mrs Rowntree," said Charles. "I have tried to find out about him, but there's no news. I'm so sorry. That isn't what you wanted to hear."

Mimi smiled sadly. "So nice to meet you, Captain Wednesday-Croft. If you'll excuse me, I must get on with my work." She drifted away.

"What is this Wednesday-Croft business?" he said.

I smiled now. "Elsie, my maid. She doesn't always concentrate. Charles, if the FANY wouldn't give you my address, how did you find me?"

"After I left the office on my last visit," he explained, "a very nice woman followed me and we had a little chat. She decided to give me your address."

Aunt Leonora! Oh, bless her!

24th December

Charles stayed for lunch and tea that day, and we talked and talked. I asked him what he did before the war. He's a writer! How exciting, I thought, until he told me he writes textbooks for schools. That must be a little dreary, but he doesn't seem to think so. He can't wait to get back to it.

He asked me what I like to do. I decided to be honest, so I told him I didn't really like doing all the usual things ladies do, like sewing and embroidery and running a house. "I like riding and swimming," I said, "and long walks with Billie." I didn't mention that I like to sing.

"I like riding and swimming, too," he said, "and I'm sure I'd love to go for long walks with your dog." He hesitated. "And with you."

Today Charles came again and we took that walk. Because of my stupid leg we only went as far as the rose garden to look at the topiary bushes, but it was heaven.

This beastly war has taken my papa, and I must accept that it has taken Archie, too. But it has given me so much. I've found that there is more to life than the things I was brought up to do. I have found a group of women who think much as

I do – who like the same things as me. I no longer feel like a square peg in a round hole. We are all pegs of very different shapes, and we must all find the hole that fits.

Mimi will learn to live with her sorrow, I know. She has her work, and it will be her support. Aunt Eloise will, I hope, sell her home on the coast and stay with us. Freddie and May adore her, and she's much better at running the house than Mimi. (Or me!)

And now I feel so warm and comfortable. Charles cares for me very much, and oh, I care for him, too. When he slipped his arm around my shoulders as we walked, I leaned on him.

This, I thought to myself, *this* is where I belong.

Historical note

In the early 1900s, a British soldier had a brilliant idea which would change the lives of many young women who might otherwise never have known adventure or danger.

Sergeant-Major Edward Charles Baker, a cavalryman, knew that many soldiers who were injured in battle died from lack of help before they could be taken back to base for treatment. Others lay in agony until help arrived. He imagined a corps of nurses on horseback, galloping to give first aid to the wounded. They'd wear scarlet tunics and would ride side-saddle, of course, because of their long skirts.

Not everyone could join the organization, because the young women had to finance themselves. They paid ten shillings to join, and six shillings a month from then onwards, and they had to supply their own uniform. It wasn't to be easy for them. They had to qualify as first-aiders and study horsemanship, learn to look after and treat horses, be disciplined, and learn other military skills, such as signalling. Many middle-class and upper-class girls, expecting to get married and live out their lives running a home and raising children, jumped at the chance to do something different.

Sergeant-Major Baker intended that his troop of young women, the First Aid Nursing Yeomanry, should be ready and waiting for the government to call on in times of war or emergency. And when war did break out in 1914, the FANY, as they were known, offered their services. Being told that as they were women they should "go home and sit still" made no difference to them. The FANY "girls", as they called themselves, weren't the type to give up, and if the British didn't want them, they would simply offer their services elsewhere. The Belgians were very happy to have their help. Eventually, their huge contribution was recognized, and the British were delighted to have the FANY working alongside the fighting forces.

By the time the war broke out, things had changed. There'd been a huge growth in the motor-car industry, and now it was clear that the FANY would not be galloping anywhere to help. They'd be driving.

During the war years of 1914–1918, the FANY drove ambulances, ran hospitals, set up canteens, enabled filthy, exhausted soldiers to have the hot bath they must have dreamed of for weeks, and performed countless other tasks such as ferrying soldiers, nurses, German prisoners and even hospital laundry around. They took great pride in doing anything that was asked of them.

The members of the FANY had a great deal of fun living and working together, but they all threw themselves into whatever task was at hand. They were known for being hard-working – carrying on until they were absolutely exhausted – and for their good humour and courage. Their bravery earned them many medals and decorations from the French and Belgians, as well as the British.

The Second World War provided plenty of new opportunities for the FANY. The organization spread far and wide, and included members from many parts of the world. The old First World War ambulances were replaced with faster – and slightly more comfortable! – vehicles, and even motorbikes. The girls' talents were recognized and used wherever necessary, often in confidential work and in deciphering codes. Some were employed in highly secret activities by the Special Operations Executive, who were responsible for secret agents sent to France. Some of the best-known of these were Odette Hallowes, Noor Inayat Khan, and Violette Szabo. In spite of being tortured by the enemy, Odette Hallowes survived the war, but many died. These women, like other FANY members, were trained in wireless communications, and their reports were vital to the progress of the war, and to the safety of many individuals.

Today the FANY has a new name – the Princess Royal's Volunteer Corps. But it's known as FANY(PRVC) so the old name hasn't been lost. The "girls" are still ready and willing in times of emergency. After a horrendous underground train crash, FANY members rushed to help the police with communications. After the sinking of a river boat, the collapse of a tower block – any major disaster – the FANY responds. On 7 July 2005, when several bombs exploded in London within an hour of each other, the FANY were called upon. They responded, working long hours with the city police. After an incident, there may be thousands of calls from anxious people, worried about family or friends. The FANY are trained to staff casualty bureaux, taking a great burden from the police.

The members of FANY are all still volunteers. Their training continues every week in areas such as first aid, navigation, communications, how to respond to a major emergency, weaponry and – of course – driving.

Timeline

1914

28 June Archduke Franz Ferdinand, the heir to the Austro-Hungarian throne, is assassinated. This was the trigger for the First World War.

28 July Austria-Hungary declares war on Serbia.

1 Aug Germany declares war on Russia.

3 August Germany declares war on France.

4 August Germany invades Belgium.

Britain declares war on Germany.

6 August Austria-Hungary declares war on Russia.

Serbia declares war on Germany.

10 August France declares war on Austria-Hungary.

12 August Britain declares war on Austria-Hungary.

23 August Germans attack the British in Belgium, at the Battle of Mons.

6 September Battle of the Marne begins in France.

Mid-October First Battle of Ypres, between the British and the Germans, begins.

November/December Britain's east coast shelled by German ships.

25 December Soldiers on the Western Front enjoy an unofficial Christmas truce; carols, presents, international football games.

1915

19 January First Zeppelin air raid on Britain.

February German U-boats (submarines) ordered to sink any ships in British waters.

April/May Second Battle of Ypres. Germans use poisonous chlorine gas.

7 May British liner *Lusitania* sunk by U-boat. Almost 1,200 people die, at least 120 of them Americans, prompting outrage in the US.

1916

February Germans attack the French, starting the Battle of Verdun, which lasts until November.

31 May Battle of Jutland, a sea battle between the British and the Germans.

1 July The Battle of the Somme begins, and lasts until November. On the first day, nearly 60,000 British soldiers are killed or injured.

15 September The British use tanks for the first time on the Western Front in the Somme battle. They're heavy and slow and many break down or get stuck in the mud.

28 November First daylight raid on London by German bombers.

5 December British Prime Minister Herbert Asquith resigns, and is replaced by David Lloyd George.

1917

6 April The United States declares war on Germany.

11 June King Constantine of Greece goes into exile and abdicates. He's succeeded by his son, Alexander, who is pro-British.

27 June Greece joins the Allies in war.

17 July King George V changes the surname of the Royal family. Instead of Saxe-Coburg-Gotha, which sounds German, he chooses Windsor for all the UK descendants of Queen Victoria.

31 July Start of the third Battle of Ypres, also known as Passchendaele.

6 November Passchendaele falls to the Allies, bringing the third Battle of Ypres to a close.

1918

15 July Second Battle of the Marne.

16–17 July Tsar Nicholas II, the Tsarina and their children, who've been captives in Siberia for months, are murdered by Bolshevik Communists.

7–11 November Germany discusses plans for an armistice

– an agreement to end the war – in a railway carriage at Compiègne, France.

9 November Kaiser Wilhelm II, the German Emperor, abdicates. Germany becomes a republic – the country no longer has a monarch.

11 November At the eleventh hour of the eleventh day of the eleventh month the armistice comes into force. The War is ended.

Picture acknowledgments

P 184   (top) Illustration of FANYs from Le Petit Journal 28/3/1909, Mary Evans Picture Library.

P 187   (bottom) First Aid Nursing Yeomanry Corps, 1917, TopFoto.co.uk/ Topham Picturepoint.

P 188   (top) Three nurses standing outside their ambulance c 1914-1918, Science & Society Picture Library/NMeM Daily Herald Archive.

P 188   (bottom) First Aid Nursing Yeomanry Corps, 1917, TopFoto.co.uk/ Topham Picturepoint.

All other pictures reproduced by the kind permission of the trustees of the Imperial War Museum, London.

LE REVEIL DU SENTIMENT MILITARISTE EN ANGLETERRE
Exercices d'ambulancières volontaires

Early members of the First Aid Nursing Yeomanry training in Britain in 1909.

Ambulance drivers maintaining their vehicles.

A bright, snowy day – but driving ambulances at night in cold weather was harsh and exhausting.

These members of FANY Unit 7 enjoy several days rest before being sent to a new post.

Ambulances had to be clean and ready to go at a moment's notice.

Pets were popular with the FANY. One convoy owned, between them, several dogs, cats and canaries, as well as a magpie.

Fur coats were greatly appreciated by the FANY on night drives in freezing winter weather.

Turning the starting handle was a hard, but necessary, chore all FANYs had to perform.

Ready for action.

A cushion or two helped to make the driving seat a little more comfortable.

Experience history first-hand with My Story –
a series of vividly imagined accounts of life in the past.

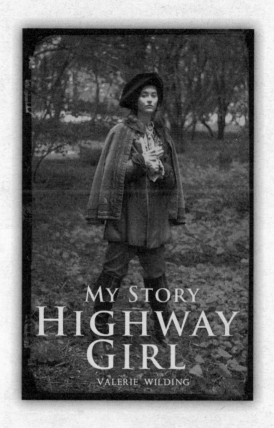

MY STORY
HIGHWAY
GIRL
VALERIE WILDING

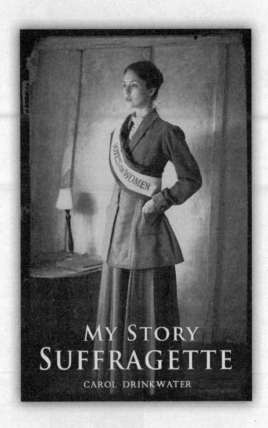

MY STORY
SUFFRAGETTE
CAROL DRINKWATER